take it to the Xtreme

SURF ZONE

Pam Withers

WALRUS
BOOKS

Walrus Books
A Division of Whitecap Books Ltd.
Second Printing 2006

Edited by Carolyn Bateman
Proofread by Joan Tetrault
Cover and interior design by Roberta Batchelor
Cover photograph by Jeremy Koreski
Typeset by Jacqui Thomas

Printed and bound in Canada

Library and Archives Canada Cataloguing in Publication

Withers, Pam
    Surf Zone / Pam Withers.

(Take it to the extreme)
ISBN 1-55285-718-2
ISBN 978-1-55285-718-2
    I. Title. II. Series: Withers, Pam. Take it to the extreme.
PS8595.I8453S97 2005   jC813'.6   C2005-902933-1

The publisher acknowledges the support of the Canada Council for
the Arts and the Cultural Services Branch of the Government of British
Columbia for our publishing program. We acknowledge the financial
support of the Government of Canada through the Book Publishing
Industry Development Program for our publishing activities.

We are committed to protecting the environment and to the responsible use of natural resources.
We are acting on this commitment by working with suppliers and printers to phase out our use
of paper produced from ancient forests. This book is printed by Webcom on 100% recycled
(40% post-consumer) paper, processed chlorine free and printed with vegetable-based inks. We
are working with Markets Initiative (www.oldgrowthfree.com) on this project.

Dedicated to the Surfrider Foundation,
which works for the "preservation and enjoyment of the world's
·oceans, waves, and beaches."

Contents

1   The North Pacific

They say the big ones come from underneath, not behind you. As Jake Evans lay on his surfboard, trailing gloved fingers in the sparkling water, he thought he felt the pulse of the ocean beneath him quicken.

He glanced behind him. Nothing but smooth-rising humps delivered at gentle intervals. But waves come in sets, with an occasional giant—four times the size of prevailing swells—hitting now and again. For the past half-hour, the late-August North Pacific had been serving up waist-high rollers packed with friendly challenge. For all of that time, he and several dozen other surfers bobbing like contented seals in this cold bay had caught and ridden wave after playful wave.

Why did Jake's sixth sense say the game was about to change? He glanced sideways at his best buddy, Peter Montpetit, whose wet blond curls bobbed over his black wetsuit. Jake was a little embarrassed to be wearing an ancient yellow wetsuit that stood out from everyone else's black ones. Unfortunately, it was the only one left on the rack by the time he'd gotten around to suiting up.

"Isn't this awesome?" Peter shouted as he sprawled his lanky body on his fancy new shortboard, flashed a big grin, and paddled lazily toward Jake.

Jake was about to reply when his instincts ordered him to swivel his board shoreward and put his arms into frantic motion. He saw Peter's mouth fall open a little when an unannounced tower of water seemed to burst from the depths. As Peter pointed the front of his board down and dove deep under the breaking wave, Jake felt his own board lift and shoot forward. In one swift move, he was up, crouched, and hurtling ahead of the rising ridge's shadow.

Go, go, go, he heard his brain scream as he tasted the salty spray from the crest just overhead and strummed the solid wall of water with the tips of his fingers. Up and down the rising slope he twisted and turned, breathing hard, determined not to be caught by the whitewater rushing at his heels. Only speed and luck would shoot him down the line before the wave collapsed and sent him tumbling. Speed, luck, and total focus. His instincts had served him well for catching this beast, but he knew the wave was as likely to tumble him as it was to tolerate his dubious hold on it.

Again, he sensed the wave walling up and starting to pitch before it closed out. With one last carve on the face, he powered up and over the wave, kicking out into midair and flying down to greet the deep green water behind.

Looking toward the beach, he saw the beast throw itself into the shallows and disintegrate into seething foam, as if despondent at failing to thrash him. He noted with satisfaction that only one other surfer had positioned herself in time to ride out the surprise berm of seawater. He squinted at her faraway figure as she gave him a thumb's up before catching a belly ride gracefully through the soup to shore.

As Jake turned and paddled back toward Peter, he felt warm and glowing even in the body-numbing cold for which Vancouver Island's west coast waters are known. He was pleased because that surfer girl's small gesture was the first time any of the other surfers had so much as acknowledged him and Peter. Not that this surprised him. Surfers are as fiercely territorial as sea lions, and even though the little Canadian town of Tofino, British Columbia, all but depended on surfing tourists to keep its economy afloat, who could blame the regulars at this cove for wanting to keep the area to themselves?

"Nice, Jake, old buddy. How the heck did you know that one was coming?" Peter greeted him as he drew near. "That was so sick. I can't believe I missed the wave of the day. I swear you're psychic or something. Everyone else got cleaned up by that one."

"One got it."

"Yeah, well, that's just one out of …" his hand gestured to all the surfers spread out along the cove, "… at least thirty here, bro. Showed them, didn't you? Maybe they'll even start speaking to us now."

Jake smiled. "To us, Peter, or to me?" It was so rare to outshine Peter at any sport, even just on one wave for a ten-second ride, that Jake couldn't resist the chance to tease his ever-exuberant friend. It was also amazing he'd aced Peter, given that Peter had honed his surf skills during Californian and Hawaiian vacations with his dad, an airline pilot, and his mom, a flight attendant. Given his parents' jobs, it seemed like Peter could fly almost anywhere for free, and his parents were well-off enough to rent him whatever boards he wanted when near a beach.

Or maybe, Jake smirked, it's just that they were keen to get rid of him for a few hours' peace now and again. Though Jake and Peter shared a high level of energy and love of sports and adventure, Peter's hyperactivity and motor-mouthing sure could get on anyone's nerves.

"Hey, Peter, who cares who talks to us and who doesn't? We'll be pulling up anchor again before anyone has a chance."

"I guess," Peter agreed, frowning. "Wish we'd stay in one place for a little while." He glanced at his waterproof watch. "Hey! We're due in the boat's galley in an hour. Better make this wave the last one."

This time, they paddled forward in synch, rose as the wave peaked, and rode the A-frame in opposite directions, Jake going left and Peter going right, hooting and hollering as each of them raced the peeling wave along the length of the beach. Not for the first time, Jake wondered if anything in the world could be as satisfying as catching and riding a wave.

"Whew, what a sweet spot! I'm so stoked. If this was California, there'd be hundreds of surfers crowding these waves," Peter was rambling as they picked up their boards and strode through the receding current's strong drag against their ankles. "Too bad we have to work tomorrow. I could play here morning till night. In fact, I could get into living here. We could be beach bums, Jake, throw a tarp over a pile of beach logs, order pizza out here every night. Does the local pizza place deliver to the beach?"

Before Jake could reply, Peter pulled himself up extra tall as a covey of surfer girls turned to enter the water near them. With a deeper-than-usual voice,

Peter called out, "Hi there, girls. What's happening? Good surf today, hey?"

The girls peered at Peter, giggled, said "totally," and threw themselves into the water after their boards. They never even glanced at Jake, though Jake figured he and Peter both cut tall, muscular figures for their fifteen years. But Peter always had been the better looking of the two, and the self-confident smooth-talker, not to mention totally girl-crazy lately. Why any girl would fall for someone who could never stop talking was beyond Jake, but then again, since Jake's own mouth would seize up as tight as a clamshell whenever a girl looked his way, who was he to judge?

"What's for supper tonight?" Peter was asking, having moved to his third favorite topic after surfing and girls: food.

"Dunno. But Chef François always serves up something great. Way better than lukewarm pizza served in a drafty jumble of logs," Jake added. They reached the parking lot just as a wetsuited youth on a bicycle with a surfboard carrier pedaled by.

"You're probably right," Peter said as they headed toward the Sam's Adventure Tours van.

"Living aboard a sixty-three-foot yacht is the only way to go. Even if it's only for two weeks, and even if it doesn't have a hot tub on deck."

"As if we'd be allowed to soak with the customers,

anyway," Jake remarked. He peered inside the empty van. Whoever had come to pick them up had probably wandered down the beach. Jake tried the door. It was unlocked.

"Sure we would. We're esteemed junior guides," Peter said as he helped Jake pull open the back doors. The two reached for their towels and dry clothes and began peeling off their heavy wetsuits. "We help the clients suit up and lower their ocean kayaks off the yacht's rear deck every morning. We babysit them on the ocean all day, nudge them here and there within five miles of the mothership, and dazzle them with our knowledge of ocean currents and sea life and paddling techniques. If one of them capsizes, who comes to the rescue? If one of them tires their wimpy little shoulder muscles, who guides them back to the mothership so the skipper's mate can hand 'em a blanket and coffee and deck chair? And who rinses out their kayaks and wetsuits every evening while they're having cocktails? We're their heroes, Jake. They love us. Of course they'd share a hot tub with us if Captain Dylan would install one on the *Adrienne*!"

"Yeah, well, it's only his first year working for Sam's Adventure Tours, and only nine clients signed on this trip. I don't think he's earning enough to install a hot tub," Jake declared as the two finished changing. Besides, thought Jake, the captain was such an uncommunicative, severe man, it would seem out of character.

"Twelve clients as of tonight," a woman's voice declared from behind them. "Three more kayakers are joining us here in Tofino before we head south to Seattle on Monday. And what's this about a hot tub?"

Jake and Peter turned around to see Nancy Sheppard, their thirty-year-old boss at Sam's Adventure Tours and the lead guide for the summer's mothership kayak tours. She was smiling and shaking her head. "I give you boys two hours off to surf after a long day of kayak guiding and you think you need a hot tub? Sounds like this trip is spoiling you."

Jake knew she was just kidding around. "We really appreciate the two hours off, Nancy. So who are the new clients?"

"A pleasant middle-aged couple from France." She paused, eyes bright with amusement. "Oh, and their fifteen-year-old daughter. Hands off, boys. She's a customer."

Peter's eyebrows shot up. "A girl, hey? That'll be a change from gray-haired kayaker wannabes."

Nancy raised her finger as if about to deliver a lecture on attitude, then stopped and laughed lightly. "Peter, you sure know how to yank my chain, don't you? You know, if you weren't so good at charming the cheeks off all our well-paying gray-haired clients,

I'd assign the first mate to keelhaul you right now for that remark. You do know what keelhauling is, right?"

"Um, where they used to half-drown anyone on a ship who misbehaved?"

"Close. Dutch navy captains used to discipline sailors by attaching them to ropes on pulleys, tossing them overboard on one side of the ship, and then hauling them up on the other side after they'd banged against the keel. With weights on their legs, no wetsuits, over barnacles, and in winter, for your information. Anyway, just throw those wetsuits in that plastic bin in the back, and hop in so we're not late for dinner. Never keep Chef François waiting. You can tell me all about the waves on the way back to the marina."

"You betcha!" the boys replied, sliding their surfboards into their bags and pushing them carefully into the van.

"And you can tell us more about this girl," Peter spoke up.

Jake smiled as Nancy rolled her eyes and fired up the van. "Boys," she said, "you still haven't told me what you're doing on your weekend off. Shall I assume you're going to hang out here and surf? You know we give clients a two-day break from the mothership in the middle of their two-week tour. And that's the day after tomorrow. The clients will be staying at a luxury hotel here in Tofino—resting, rediscovering their 'land legs,' and shopping. And Captain Curtis Dylan and his first mate, Gavin Kelly, are taking the *Adrienne* north for some fishing and diving. So I've made tentative arrangements for the two of you to stay at a youth hostel with bus service to the beaches. I'll be staying in a bed and breakfast close to the hostel if you need me."

Jake and Peter looked at each other. When Peter didn't jump in, Jake spoke. "Yeah, Nancy, we've been talking about that, and the reason we haven't said anything is that we've been waiting to ask Captain Dylan if he'd let us stay aboard."

"Stay aboard?" Nancy looked surprised. "With just the captain and first mate? Instead of surfing here?"

"Well, the surfing's real tempting, but, as you know, Jake and I just finished our scuba diving certification this year," Peter explained. "In fact, we really appreciate your helping to arrange and pay for our course. And Captain Dylan was telling us there's some excellent diving on the west coast of Vancouver Island."

"He sometimes takes diving clients on the *Adrienne*," Jake inserted.

"Everyone says diving from a boat is the way to go, 'cause you can get to better places and it's easier, and we don't know when else we'll ever get the chance to do boat-diving together," Peter added.

"And we thought maybe he'd let us stay aboard and take us to somewhere we could dive," Jake finished, hoping his voice didn't sound like he was pleading. "We wouldn't be any bother to him and Gavin. We could maybe do some work for them when we're not diving."

"I see," Nancy said as she pulled into the marina parking lot, cut the engine, and directed her eyes on Captain Dylan. He was standing on the *Adrienne*'s deck, studying an island across the bay with an expensive pair of binoculars. "Well, I guess that's up to him. It's okay by me as long as you're back for Monday's guiding, as I know you will be."

"Thanks, Nancy!" the boys said, slapping their palms together.

But there was still the matter of whether Captain Dylan would go for it, Jake reminded himself as they walked up the gangplank toward the tall, barrel-chested, and formidably unfriendly captain.

2 Surfer Girl

A light fog seemed to have dropped gauzy curtains across the *Adrienne*'s wide salon windows the next morning, but that didn't bother Jake. He was feeling pretty good about having talked Captain Dylan into letting him and Peter stay aboard over the weekend. The captain, ever dour, had refused initially, but between them, Jake and Peter had finally won him over. Their offer of doing chores all weekend for the privilege had certainly helped.

Boat dives were way too expensive for his parents to ever pay for, so Jake saw this as his big chance. In fact, his parents could never have paid for the diving certification in the first place, but Nancy had gotten Sam's Adventure Tours to underwrite it on the chance it might be useful when the boys got enough dives logged to help out as divemasters.

"Hope this mist burns off soon so we can get on

the water," Peter grumped as he poured syrup on a stack of pancakes that would daunt most grown men.

"It'll be a long enough day as it is," Jake responded, yawning as he shook some pepper on his three-egg omelet. "Nancy says we're each to lead a group of six, and she'll paddle back and forth between us."

"Yeah? And who gets the new family?" Peter asked, glancing around for the umpteenth time that morning, probably in hopes of seeing the girl they'd barely gotten a glimpse of the evening before.

"I'm sure Nancy will have that worked out too," Jake replied evenly. "Oh, and she said no surfing this afternoon till after we've helped the clients move their luggage from the *Adrienne* to the hotel."

"Bummer. Thought we were junior guides, not porters. But at least we get to see the inside of that five-star place on the beach. Hey, if we were allowed to stay there, would you have chosen that over going diving with Captain Tyrant and First Mate Suck-up?" Peter needled Jake.

Jake smirked but glanced quickly around them to make sure no one had heard their secret nicknames for the boat's operators. "Nah, we'd just feel out of place there. Bunch of super-rich tourists. This way we get a chance to see sea urchins, wolf eels, maybe even octopuses. I'd be so stoked to pet a wolf eel."

"More than one octopus is octopi, not octopuses, Jake.

And we're not supposed to touch anything, remember? It stresses them. Except maybe urchins. Hey!" he said, then paused and whistled under his breath. "Looky-here. Speaking of something we're not supposed to touch."

Jake had already seen a distinguished-looking couple enter the room with a petite girl whose long dark hair, woven through with a string of tiny beads, was wound into an elegant coil on top of her head. She wore a clingy, hand-knit sweater over tight designer jeans and high-heeled sandals. As she turned to scan the room quickly with warm brown eyes, her earrings sparkled. Her eyes rested briefly on Jake and Peter, the only other teenagers on the boat. Then, with a blink of her long lashes, she looked quickly away. But not before Jake detected a shy smile.

And not before Jake felt an uneasy spell descend on him. His pulse, like that of the ocean's yesterday, began to quicken as if something not quite under his control was about to hit. She wasn't like any girl he'd ever seen before, and certainly nothing like any girl he'd ever formed a vague crush on in the past. She was more than drop-dead gorgeous. She was, well, totally classy. And frighteningly mesmerizing. He tore his eyes away to see Peter's eyes narrowed on him.

"Out of bounds, old buddy," Peter was saying, but whether he was speaking to Jake or reminding himself,

Jake couldn't be sure.

Just then Chef François hustled out of his galley and beelined straight to the new family.

"*Je suis tellement heureuse de rencontrer un français,*" he said.

Such a pleasure to meet a fellow countryman, Jake interpreted to himself with a bit of a struggle.

"*Je suis très contente de vous rencontrer, Chef. J'ai entendu tellement de compliments de votre cuisine.*" A pleasure to meet you, Chef. I've heard glowing reports of your cuisine, the girl's father had replied, standing to kiss the chef first on one cheek, then the other, then the first again.

Jake looked at Peter. Peter looked at Jake. "French," they said together.

"Parisian French," Jake added thoughtfully after a minute. Quebecois French people definitely had a harsher accent. And now that he thought about it, these folks looked European—as in, a little too fashionable for an adventure cruise on a stopover in Tofino, whose population was 1,800 not counting any bears, wolves, cougars, killer whales, or tourists. By some standards, he mused, Tofino was about as far away from an urban center as one could get these days. Until a few years ago, it was one of the surfing world's best-kept secrets. Now, the community hosted a national surf event every year.

Jake searched his brain quickly for anything he knew about France. Lots of ocean. Some world-class surfers and divers. Great food, wine, and chefs. Warm weather, girls in bikinis, and the Eiffel Tower. Hmmm, that was a pretty shallow list. But it's not like he'd had a chance to think much about it. He'd come up with other things as the day went on, wouldn't he?

"Jake, Peter!" Jake only just realized that it was the second time Nancy had spoken their names, and she was standing right beside their table. "Come meet Dr. and Mrs. Chambre, and their daughter Valerie."

Valerie, thought Jake. Yes, introduce me to Valerie. The boys rose and followed closely behind Nancy as Chef François trotted back to the galley, humming.

"Dr. Chambre, Mrs. Chambre, and Valerie, this is Jake Evans and Peter Montpetit, my assistant kayak guides. Jake and Peter, Dr. and Mrs. Chambre are curators at a museum in Bayonne, France—that's on the southwest coast near the Spanish border—and this is their daughter."

"So pleased to meet you," Dr. Chambre said in a smooth French accent as he stood to shake their hands. "We are so looking forward to ocean kayaking in British Columbia. And Peter, you are French, no?"

Jake watched Valerie's face lift to Peter's with interest.

"Um, no. Well, somewhere back in the family, I suppose. I'm American, from Seattle, Washington."

"Ah, but you know of course that Montpetit means 'little mountain'?"

"Um, yes, of course," Peter stumbled a bit, shaking hands with the older Chambres and Valerie.

"And you are Jake," Dr. Chambre said, turning to Jake. "You are from America or Canada?"

"*Je suis canadien et je suis très heureux de faire votre connaissance.*" I'm Canadian and I'm very pleased to meet you. Jake spoke confidently but still couldn't look directly at Valerie. He'd gotten an A in French last semester. Might as well put it to some use. "*Je vis à Chilliwack en Colombie-Britannique à l'est de Vancouver. Nous avons beaucoup de montagnes, rivières, forêts, et lacs là bas.*" I live in Chilliwack, British Columbia, east of Vancouver. We have lots of mountains, rivers, forest, and lakes there.

"*Très bon. Votre français est parfait,*" Mrs. Chambre said. Very good. Your French is perfect. "Chilliwack sounds beautiful."

"Yes, perhaps we should visit there before we fly out of Vancouver," Valerie added in English with a warm smile. This effectively choked off any further supply of French from Jake.

Peter, who wasn't very good at French, looked clearly annoyed.

"After breakfast," Nancy inserted, "Jake and Peter will find you some wetsuits that fit, and assign you some kayaks. They'll also show you the launch deck. We hope to be on the water in two hours if visibility allows."

"Hopefully this fog will lift," Peter said, looking from Valerie to her parents as if fearful Nancy would dismiss him.

"Of course it will lift," Valerie spoke softly. "Did you see reddish clouds at sunset last night? It means will be clear before noon. Perhaps you know English saying, 'Red sky at night, sailor's delight'?"

"'Red sky at morning, sailor's warning,'" Peter finished off for her with a bold wink.

Nancy laughed. "Is there a French version that also rhymes? And are you a sailor, Valerie?"

"*En française*, we say, '*Ciel rouge le soir, la pluie en retard*,'" Valerie responded in her pleasant accent. "I am many times on sailing boats, but mostly I am surfer."

"Well, there is certainly some great surfing around Tofino, but it's a lot colder than in France. You need thick wetsuits here—and hoods and gloves in winter—isn't that right, boys? I'm sure they'd show you the ropes this weekend, but they're off north to do some diving instead."

"Diving? I also dive. There is good diving north of here?"

"Excellent diving and surfing," Gavin, the short, trim, and excessively polite ship's first mate spoke up as he approached. "You were enjoying some local surf yesterday, Valerie, your parents were saying."

Jake watched Gavin adjust his bow tie, a ridiculous thing for a first mate to wear, even in the salon at mealtime. But from what Jake had seen, Gavin loved being a fashion statement.

"On Chesterman's Beach," she replied.

Jake studied her closely. "You were there around five o'clock? You caught that big set wave?"

"*Oui*, Jake, like you," she said.

Jake felt his face grow warm, saw Peter cross his arms. Hmmm, so there was some advantage to being the only one wearing an old yellow wetsuit.

"You will please to tell me more about the diving later?" Valerie asked Jake and Peter. Chef François hovered with plates of omelets, croissants, and fruit salad complete with sprigs of parsley. He shooed the boys, Nancy, and Gavin away from his new clients' table.

"You bet!" Peter said as they backed away.

"*Bon appetit!*" Gavin called out, turning his polished shoes toward the chart room.

3   The Junior Guides

After breakfast, Jake and Peter threw themselves into their morning guide duties, gathering gear and answering clients' questions. It wasn't until half the group was safely launched in their seventeen-foot kayaks that Nancy informed them Valerie had been assigned to Jake's group and her parents to Peter's. Jake was careful to hide his smile as Peter's face reflected fury for a split second.

It took all of Jake's nerve to address himself to Valerie, even though she seemed friendly. He noticed that her hair now formed a neat bun at the nape of her neck.

"So, have you ever been in a kayak before?" he asked, eyes struggling to stay on her face.

"No, but always I want to try one," she replied, beaming.

"Okay, I'll take you through the basics, and I'll keep

an eye out for you. We'll be close to shore most of the time, and we never get into anything more than gentle waves. Probably nothing to worry about."

She nodded, and Jake thought her eyes sparkled like the water that was splashing playfully against their hulls. Get a grip, he said to himself, then showed her the best way to hold her paddle and the most efficient way to stroke. Then he pointed to the sprayskirt designed to keep water out of her boat.

"If you flip over, just pull on the sprayskirt's grab-loop and you'll come out of the boat easily. I'll be right there to rescue you," he said. "But don't worry; these kayaks are very stable."

"So we paddle several kilometer along *la plage*, the beach, and have picnic lunch, and then *La Adrienne* comes to find us?" she asked.

"That's right," Jake assured her. "Or I can radio for the *Adrienne*'s motorized dinghy sooner if you get tired."

"Not me," she laughed. "I love it already. I think I can paddle all day."

Judging from how she'd surfed yesterday, Jake guessed she probably could.

"Look! An eagle," a nearby client shouted, setting his paddle down across his lap to lift his binoculars to his eyes. The group watched the eagle soar and circle gracefully.

"They have six-foot wingspans and their nests can weigh a ton: as much as a mini-van," Jake informed the group. The six kayakers nodded their heads like respectful students in a class. Jake was suddenly pleased that Nancy had taught them about bird and marine life in the area, though it had seemed long and boring at the time. "Eagle nests," he informed them, "are very comfortable inside, lined with mosses and lichens."

The clients paddled for an hour, oohing and ahhing at the seagulls, cormorants, and oystercatchers that swooped overhead. When one client spotted a jellyfish just below the ocean's surface and tried to lift it with his paddle, Jake sprinted over.

"Not a good idea, sir," he advised. "Not just because it can damage the jellyfish, but also because some types of jellyfish in this area can sting, even through a wetsuit glove."

"Oh!" he heard Valerie exclaim behind him, prompting him to pull some strong sweep turns to paddle back to her. From the corner of his eye, he saw a baby seal plop back into the water beside her.

"It nearly landed on kayak!" she said. "It leaped up into the air. It scared me!"

Jake grinned. "Just a harmless harbor seal pup. It's unusual to see seals jump like that. You're lucky. Guess it just wanted a closer look at you. Keep an eye out.

It'll pop up again in a minute or two. Even the grown seals don't stay underwater for more than a few minutes at a time."

"Only a few minutes?" a red-haired woman asked as she adjusted her designer sunglasses.

"Well, if they have to, they can stay submerged for half an hour."

"Yes, and they'll sometimes nap on the ocean floor where it's shallow, just offshore," Nancy added as she joined the group with strong, sure strokes. "Aren't they cute? And they're very curious. There's another."

The group turned and saw large, dark eyes on a round, smooth head studying them intently. The tiny nose sported a thick set of whiskers, and freckles seemed to run up its face. Jake could swear it was smiling. He saw Valerie try to creep up behind it, but he knew the shy seal would disappear soundlessly into the aqua water long before she came within reach.

"*Très jolie!*" Valerie ruled. "Very pretty."

"Hey, Peter's group is getting pretty far ahead," Nancy teased them. "Guess who's going to get most of the avocado salad for *dîner* if we don't get a move on?"

Peter was standing just off the beach, up to his knees in water, catching the bow of each kayak as people landed. He helped pull each boat up far enough that clients didn't have to get their feet wet when they climbed out.

"Such service!" Dr. Chambre laughed.

"I'm fine, *merci*," Valerie said cheerfully as Peter tried to offer her a hand.

Soon the boys were busy helping Nancy spread the picnic cloth on a long, flat rock and setting out plates and platters of food.

Half an hour later, as the two groups were beach-combing along the shore and photographing tidal pools, Peter picked up a long stalk of bull kelp. With a wicked grin, he broke off its softball-sized bulb and tossed it at Jake.

"You're pitcher. I'm batter," he declared. "Valerie, ever played baseball?"

She paused from skipping rope with another long stalk of bull kelp. "*Jamais*. Never. Teach me!"

The clients gathered around as Peter kept swinging his wavering yellow "bat" at the "ball" that Jake slung his way. He managed a few hits that Valerie chased after. Someone started shaping piles of seaweed into bases, and soon the game was in full swing.

Everyone took a turn, and a few, including Nancy and Valerie, even managed to make the slimy stalk connect with its former head.

"Yuck!" someone shouted as a hard whack cracked the bulb open before it rolled in the sand.

"There's a whole lot more bats and balls where that came from," the gentleman birdwatcher observed, pointing to the endless piles of kelp stretching along the shore as far as they could see.

"And entire forests of it underwater," Jake told him. "The stalks get up to six stories tall. When we pass floating kelp beds in the ocean, look for the sea otters that live in them."

"I would like to see *l'outre*!" Valerie said.

"Well, keep your eyes open," Nancy told her. "Shall we head out again, folks?"

"*Impossible*. My parents are not yet come," said Valerie.

Heads swung around as Dr. and Mrs. Chambre came strolling up the beach, talking animatedly about an object that Dr. Chambre cupped protectively in his hands.

"A glass ball!" Nancy observed. "That's a real find. Japanese fishermen used to use them to keep their nets afloat, and until a few years ago, they were fairly common along the West Coast. Now they're rare."

"And valuable?" Dr. Chambre asked, eyebrows raised as he looked to Nancy.

"Valuable, yes. But more important, they're supposed to bring good luck," she told him.

Instead of smiling, the museum professionals looked disappointed with her reply. "How valuable?" they pressed.

Nancy's dark eyes surveyed them carefully and she shrugged. "I don't know." She reached out to touch the glass ball, but Dr. Chambre pulled it slightly away from her reach.

Jake then watched as the man wrapped the ball in his fleece jacket as if he were swaddling a newborn baby and tucked it into his kayak.

4   To the Rescue

After lunch, the twelve kayakers and three guides paddled for almost two hours before they rounded a point and spotted the *Adrienne* anchored and waiting for them. Small waves were kicking up between them and the yacht. Despite the warm sun and the wetsuits they wore, a few of the clients were beginning to shiver. He, Peter, and Nancy could have sprinted to the *Adrienne* in five minutes flat, but the tourists they were herding toward the sloop·would take twenty, he calculated. He pulled back to make sure he could keep everyone in sight. The chop lifted and slapped his boat down noisily, as if inviting him to play.

Valerie, paddling with strong strokes just behind Nancy, was way up at the front. A gray-haired woman wearing a floppy sunhat was the last in Jake's group. He amused himself by watching the brim of the sunhat flap up and down with the breeze and bobbing waves. The poor woman was pulling on her paddle like someone trying to lift weights for the first time. She'd be the most relieved to reach the mothership.

As he raised his eyes to the group's frontrunners again, he saw Valerie veer and head sharply away from shore. What on earth was she up to? The rest of the group ignored her, following Nancy's lead toward the yacht.

Jake shouted to Valerie, hoping the noise would at least alert Nancy to look behind her, but the wind took his words and scattered them. Only the woman with the floppy sunhat looked around, startled.

"Carry on," he told her. "I'll be right back." And he began sprinting toward Valerie, who was getting into larger waves.

"Valerie!" he shouted again as he drew close, but she either couldn't or wouldn't hear. Now he saw where she was headed: a tiny rock outcrop covered with sea lions. No you don't, he thought. Seals are cute. Sea lions are not. Seals are harmless. Sea lions are very, very territorial. Not to mention they're almost as long as a compact car and weigh up to a ton. Though he could recall only one recorded incident of a sea lion deliberately tipping over a sea kayaker, Jake wasn't about to let Valerie test this colony's annoyance level.

Splash! Splash! One by one, the sea lions, disturbed by Valerie's approach, were hurling themselves off the island and disappearing below the water's surface. The deep roars and growls of the remaining herd members made such a racket even Valerie was slowing. Jake glanced back at the rest of the kayakers. Nancy was monitoring the situation from the small deck at the rear of the sloop called a swim grid as she helped clients aboard one by one. Peter's group was nearing the *Adrienne*, although clearly distracted by what Jake and Valerie were up to. Jake knew Peter wouldn't dare leave his assigned group, much as he probably wanted to paddle over and be the one to divert Valerie.

"Valerie. Back away. Sea lions aren't like seals," Jake shouted, sure she could hear him this time. They were so close that the stench of the island filled his nostrils, and the animals' roars hurt his ears. "They could knock your kayak over! "

He didn't mean to scare her. He knew the sea mammals, uneasy as they were about her encroaching on their territory, were highly unlikely to do such a thing. But he needed to stop her from trying to land on their island. They were sure to become more aggressive if she set foot on their rock.

Unfortunately, his words froze her hands in mid-stroke. Now she was just sitting there, only a few kayak lengths away from the creatures who hadn't dived yet. And her boat was drifting sideways alongside the island, bobbing in the small waves crashing against it.

"Valerie!" he shouted as he sprinted even closer to her. "Back away or turn around!"

She twisted her body to look at him, panic on her face. She stuck her paddle in the water as if ready to arc her boat around, then leaned hard on it. Oops. The blade sank through the water like a knife cutting lemon meringue pie. The boat tipped, and into the drink went Valerie.

Jake cranked his arms as fast as they'd go to paddle his kayak to her side. He looked down into the water and saw her body and long arms flailing just under the surface like a mirage. She's trying to find the loop on her sprayskirt to pull it and eject, he thought. But if I can reach her hands first ... The cold of the water shocked him as he plunged his own arms deeply into it. He grabbed her cold, panicked hands and gritted his teeth as he swung her up far enough that she could grab a breath. Her arms were wrapped around his like octopus tentacles, her face upturned, her eyes bugged out.

He smiled to reassure her as his knees gripped his kayak's kneepads to counter her weight. Her boat was tilted halfway between upright and upside down. Her head and chest lay on the water's surface as she gasped and he held on tight.

"Keep hold of my arms and swing your hips a little more to bring the boat all the way back upright," he instructed her, working his knees harder to prevent her from pulling him over.

One, two, three tries and she and her boat completed the maneuver. "How—how—how'd you do that?" she sputtered, eyes wide.

"You helped me. We rolled you up so you wouldn't eject and swim too close to the sea lions," he explained. "Good thing you're lightweight or I couldn't have pulled that off."

"Th-thank you." Her eyes moved back to the seal's island warily.

He raised a finger to push back strands of wet hair plastered against her cheeks as she blinked at him.

"Sorry. I'm sorry, Jake. I didn't know. I just wanted closer look at them ..."

"It's okay," he said, scanning the dark water around them, expecting whiskered brown heads to rise and give them the evil eye. "Just turn around slowly and follow me. And don't look at them directly. Sea lions are extremely territorial. They regard kayaks as a threat if they come too close." He repeated the information in French to make sure she understood.

"What happens if I come out of the boat and they are around me under the water?" she asked breathlessly as the two drew close to the *Adrienne*. She paused to pull her hair back into a neat ponytail and compose herself. Her big, appealing eyes were on his face.

"Probably nothing," Jake said. "But that's not something we'd want to test. I guess you're not likely to go sprinting off from the group again anytime soon." He didn't like having to chastise her, but, hey, it was his job to keep everyone safe, and Nancy would expect him to give her some kind of gentle reprimand. He also knew that if Valerie had swum out of her overturned boat, Peter or Nancy would have been over in a shot to help him rescue her.

Valerie hung her head. "No. I am really sorry. You are good guide, Jake. *Merci encore.* Thanks again."

Jake smiled. He had an urge to take her hands and squeeze them, just to reassure her, but even if he'd thought Valerie would be okay with that, his own shyness wouldn't let him. Besides, as they took up paddles again and headed toward the yacht, he realized that Peter, Nancy, and her parents were grouped along the sloop's railing, watching anxiously.

He and Valerie were startled by clapping from above as they reached the *Adrienne*, and he helped her onto the swim grid. But as the two made their way to the deck, he saw Captain Dylan walking forcefully toward them. Jake was pretty sure he'd done okay out there, given the situation, but a part of him felt like cowering as the big man halted in front of them, blocking their way. The rest of the crowd fell silent.

"Lad, you handled that very well indeed," his deep voice boomed. Jake relaxed a little. Captain Dylan was a man of few words and even fewer compliments.

"Young lady," he added, turning to Valerie, "please come see Nancy and me in the library in an hour. We need to have a talk about safety and protocol."

Valerie nodded her head nervously as her wetsuit dripped on the deck. Then the captain was gone, and Nancy, Peter, and the kayakers began pumping Jake's hand while Dr. and Mrs. Chambre rushed over to hug Valerie and spirit her away to the warmth and privacy of their cabin.

"So," Peter said an hour later, as the two were peeling and chopping onions in the galley for Chef François, "aren't you a little hero? Saved the damsel in distress from the big, bad sea lions. Next thing we know, you'll be ditching the diving to play with Surfer Girl on the weekend. Surfer Girl who noticed you catch a super-duper wave. Is that what you've got in mind?"

Jake smirked, chopped an onion in half, and raised the two ends to Peter's eyes before Peter could stop him. "Oh, poor Peter, he's crying. Just 'cause the boss assigned me to the new girl before him."

Peter's strong arms slapped the onions down and he produced a wide grin. "That's right, old buddy. She's all mine tomorrow."

"Wrongo, old buddy," Jake mimicked Peter's voice. "You've forgotten that tomorrow we leave the customers to their luxury hotel, and we heave-ho with the captain and his first mate to some mystery cove up north."

Peter's mouth dropped open a little. He had forgotten that today was Friday already. Jake took the opportunity to throw a sliver of onion at his friend. Whoa! That brilliant move cost him. Peter threw it back and soon the two were chasing each other at high speed around the galley, tossing fragments of onions until their feet slipped and they began laughing and wrestling on the floor.

"*Arrête! Arrête!* Stop!" the shrill voice of Chef François rang out as he entered the galley. "What is this foolishness? *Imbéciles!* To think you two were hired for guides to lead the peoples. You are nothing but silly children. *Ces enfants sont complètement stupides!* Out of my galley! *Allez!* Go! Oh, my poor onions!"

Jake and Peter, still laughing, shed their aprons and began to slink out, but Captain Dylan stepped into their path, his grizzled face like chiseled rock.

"Hello, lads."

"Hello, Captain Dylan," they said, straightening their shoulders as if being inspected by the principal.

"We weigh anchor at first light tomorrow. I'll expect you above-decks and sleeves rolled up then. Gavin and I have a long list of chores that need doing."

"Yes, sir."

He took a step forward, as if dismissing them silently, but paused mid-stride and looked back. "And I'll expect perfect behavior from all three of you."

"Three, sir?" Jake ventured.

"You, Peter, and Valerie," he said sternly. Despite the captain's expressionless face, Jake had the sneaking suspicion the man was enjoying the shocked look he had just produced on two boyish faces. "She's a diver," he declared, as if that explained everything. "And she argues till she gets her way, with her parents and with me, just like the two of you."

With that, he turned heel and stalked away through the narrow cockpit that held the ship's wheel, toward the companionway and his stateroom.

Jake and Peter stared at each other for a full half-minute. Then, as if someone had given them a cue, they high-fived each another and sprinted to their bunks to change. No point smelling like onions before eating dinner, moving their clients to ritzy new digs, and catching a little surf at sunset.

5   Three Surfers

"**S**urf's big this evening," Peter pronounced. He judged the waves to be hollow and just overhead, roughly the limit of what he could comfortably handle. He shivered a little as his fingers clutched the surfboard he was carrying. He and Jake had just arrived on Chesterman's and were watching sets of waves roll in as the sun slipped toward the horizon. The clients had been duly delivered to their hotel, baggage and all. They were probably watching the surfers through the big picture window in the hotel's front lounge while sipping drinks in easy chairs.

"Let's take a minute to watch what's happening out there, okay?"

"Good idea," Jake agreed as the two plopped down on the wet sand.

Peter had hoped Valerie would join them in the

water for the last hour of daylight, but she'd disappeared with her parents into town. Man, was she ever something to look at. He had it bad for her, for sure. Good thing Jake wasn't interested in girls or he'd have some competition. Well, maybe Jake got crushes and stuff, but he'd never really pursued anyone—could hardly talk to girls, in fact. Which came in handy sometimes, Peter reflected with a quick grin. Jake had tons of things going for him, and Peter would do anything for his best friend. But when it came to turning girls' heads, well, let's just say that Peter had more experience and dedication in that department.

"There's how it's done," Peter commented, pointing to a pro tearing down the line on a wave. He wished he could pull off something like that.

"Yeah, that guy's sick. He's got it happening," Jake agreed.

The two were silent as a lull settled on the row of surfers paddling about. Then Peter eyed a solid set feathering on the outside. As it reared ever higher, the sun shone through its thinnest portion, creating a kaleidoscope of colors. Peter glued his eyes on the backlit wave as it reached the would-be wave riders. Like ants in the shadow of a footstep, they suddenly spun, sprinted, and scattered. A few scrambled to the shoulder, but as the wave broke, most of the pack was pitched into the pit. Now the wave drew itself up to its full height on the inside. Peter watched with envy as one surfer carved a 360 on its steep face, and another did some fancy footwork to stay upright. Several others shot like arrows along the milky-blue walls as the rest of the set broke. Then, like all mighty waves, the last and biggest pile of water threw itself headlong onto the shallow sandbar. Peter couldn't pull his eyes away from the faint traces of bodies being tumbled under-water in the whitewash.

"Raisins in a milkshake," Jake remarked, "with the blender on high speed."

Peter laughed and slapped his mate's back. "You pick your waves, you pay your dues. Let's join 'em."

The two ran and jumped in to greet the next set. Peter cringed as the first cold wave slapped his face. There are only two challenges to surfing, he thought: getting through the shore break, and then getting to the beach without being trashed too badly. As freez-ing water crept between his skin and wetsuit, then warmed up against his body, he jumped over the small waves and dove under the large ones. Soon he and Jake reached where they wanted to be: in the lineup waiting for action.

"Hey, Jake—there's Gavin and Valerie's folks." Peter had spotted the first mate, dressed in a loud Hawaiian shirt and white trousers and sporting a cigar in one hand, seating Dr. and Mrs. Chambre in chairs on the hotel's beach-level front patio. Then the sailor sat down with them, notebook in hand, and the three bent their heads in intent discussion as Gavin began taking notes. What were they up to? Peter wondered.

Of course, he couldn't afford to look for long. He saw a wave begin to wall up behind him, positioned his board, and began stroking into position with his head turned to watch the water behind. As the smaller waves passed under him and he glanced to shore, Peter had a panoramic view of the beach's forest, thinned in places by million-dollar hotels and houses. Now the wave he'd been watching lifted him, and with some effort, he dropped into it, sprang to a crouch, then dared to stand.

Whoa. He was in the zone now. Like a bar slammed down on a carnival-ride vehicle, his board locked into the wave. He could feel the briny breath of the curl behind him, and he could see Jake up and riding directly ahead. Loosening up, he arced a little left, a little right. Nothing fancy; just little maneuvers from trough to peak and back again. When the wall beside him slowed, he cut back for more speed. When it sped up, he leaned forward, S-turned, and found the high line. When it neared the beach, he held his breath, pumped, and exploded over the top, double-grabbing his board's rails in mid-air before flying down. He passed so close to Jake that the two were able to slap hands before squirting off in different directions.

As they sank back into the water, their faces glowed with triumph. "A perfect ten," Peter ruled.

"*Magnifique!*" they heard Valerie exclaim. She was stroking toward them from the beach, her long, glistening ponytail floating beside her.

"Valerie, you made it!" Peter greeted her, delighted that she'd caught his faultless surf act. "What did you get up to in town?"

"*Bonjour,*" Jake added in what Peter considered his pathetic attempt to impress her with his school French.

"Hello, *mes guides,*" she responded with a laugh. "We went to museum of native art, and then spent too much time in the bookstore. My parents will need *un tronc* to carry so many books about West Coast archaeology home."

"Well, glad you could make it," Peter said. Then, as one of the locals whistled and started stroking seaward, he shouted, "Wave coming!"

The three slid down the first wave in the set like kids on winter sleds, legs pumping. Valerie caught the first one, and Jake and Peter the second one far enough apart to share it. All made it to their feet as the waves propelled them playfully forward. Jake raced ahead, trying moves Peter knew to be a little beyond what he could usually pull off. Peter's board, too, seemed inclined to dance fast and furiously. When Valerie popped over the back of her wave and glanced his way, he rode up and hit the lip. Even though this made him dig a rail (the equivalent of a snowboard catching an edge) and hurtled him head-first into a nasty spin-cycle, it seemed worthwhile for having made her smile that gentle French smile of hers. Never mind that she also turned it on Jake as he popped up from his own spill.

Long past when most of the surfers had exited the waves, the trio paddled, surfed, spilled, and laughed. Peter noticed that Valerie avoided the biggest waves, but never faltered on those she did choose to drop into. She was graceful as a bird, born to surf, he decided.

"So," Peter inquired as they were toweling themselves down in the hazy light of dusk, "how long have you been surfing, Valerie?"

She smiled, removed the rubber band on her pony-tail, and let her dark hair fall around her shoulders. "This I do not know. Ask my parents. We grew up beside surfing beach, so I catch rides on front of my father's board perhaps before I am four."

"It shows. You were ripping out there," Jake commented.

Ha! Peter thought. Jake almost managed to look at her and say something to her at the same time. Good on him. "So, looking forward to diving off the

Adrienne on the weekend?" Peter said, moving closer to Valerie, rolling the top of his wetsuit down, and flinging his towel around his neck casually.

"Yes. Gavin says this coast has many—how do you say?—sunken ships. This is why it is called 'Graveyard of the Pacific,' yes? Maybe he let us dive near these sunken ship?"

"I doubt that," Peter hurried to reply before Jake could. "It takes special dive training to explore underwater wrecks. Have you been diving since you were four as well?" he teased.

Valerie's smile dimmed a little, making Peter want to bite his tongue off. "No, only few years," she said. "And always with parents and instructor until this year. I now am old enough to dive without instructor."

"We use the same international rules," Jake spoke up. "Peter and I have only just finished our certification."

Peter wished Jake hadn't said it quite like that. "So, when was Gavin filling you in on local diving information?" he asked as they strolled down the beach toward her hotel, Jake in tow.

"Just now, at the gallery," she said. "My parents like him much. Perhaps this is why they decide I can go this weekend," she said.

"Oh. Yes, we're stoked about that," Peter said.

"What means 'stoked,' please?"

This set both Jake and Peter laughing, but instead

of saying "fired up and excited," Peter provided a toned-down translation: "Pleased," he said politely.

"Ah, and I am also stoked," she said, looking confused when the boys peeled into new gales of laughter.

"I see the three of you are getting along just fine," Gavin's voice greeted them from the hotel patio. Peter looked up to see him flick ashes from his cigar into an ashtray on the table in front of them. "I've just been reassuring Alexandre and Olivette here that you two are okay. At least, you are when under my supervision," he added, drawing the words out slowly, as if for the benefit of amusing his table companions. "Peter here needs a little more supervision than Jake," he added, raising one eyebrow, "but they're both decent workers, as kids go."

Peter rankled a little at the word "kids," ignored Jake's smile, and thought it a little odd that Gavin seemed to be treating the Chambres with such familiarity. He'd never heard Gavin call any of the other clients by their first names. The overly solicitous man even called Nancy, who was his age, "Miss Sheppard." Nor had Peter ever seen the first mate smoke a cigar. He wrinkled his nose at the smell of it, and saw Valerie do the same.

"Good evening, Dr. and Mrs. Chambre," Peter said. "I understand you were in the native art gallery. There's some really nice stuff there." Okay, that sounded lame, but the only time he'd ever peeked in was to warm up on a cold winter day after surfing. "I'm sure it doesn't seem like much compared with your museum in France."

"Actually, it holds excellent displays of local aboriginal art and history," Dr. Chambre said as he lifted a stemmed glass of wine to his lips. "This interests us very much."

"Father, *please*," Valerie teased him with a warning tone.

"Valerie, dear, you need to change out of that wetsuit," Mrs. Chambre spoke up. "How you can stand such freezing water …" she added, setting down her lipstick-stained glass and picking up the room key from their table. She handed it to Valerie. "Hotel has a sauna, steam room, and hot tub. Go get warm, *ma chère*," she advised her daughter.

Peter half hoped she'd extend the sauna, steam room, and hot tub invitation to him and Jake, but between her silence and Gavin's look, he figured out that wasn't going to happen.

"Well, I guess we had better get back to the boat," Jake suggested. "Nice to meet you again, Dr. and Mrs. Chambre. Enjoy your weekend, and I look forward to seeing you on Monday. Valerie, good surfing with you."

"Stoked," she teased back, waving at both him and Peter before turning and heading into the hotel.

Peter knew better than to watch her retreat while her parents' and Gavin's eyes were on him, tempting as it was to watch her cute figure disappear into the glow of the luxury hotel.

"Enjoy your evening," he said as politely as he could to her mother and father. "And see you on Monday."

"*Au revoir,*" Dr. Chambre returned, while accepting a cigar from Gavin. "Enjoy your diving."

"Yes, be very careful while diving, Peter and Jake," Mrs. Chambre chimed in. Then she lifted her wine-glass. "A toast to our junior guides. *A lundi.* Until Monday."

6   Up the Coast

When Jake and Peter crawled out of their narrow bunks the next morning, the *Adrienne* was already slicing silently through the water. Jake yawned, stretched, and pulled on a lightweight sweater as Peter bumped into him hopping on one foot and trying to stick the other into his jeans.

"Wonder how long we've been underway." Jake peeked out the porthole at the rugged, mist-enshrouded coastline. "And how far north we're going."

"I asked the captain and Gavin that question last night, and neither one bothered to answer me," Peter complained. "But look on the chart table. Lots of inlets and fjords and islands. Some population, but not tons."

Jake looked out the porthole again at dense forest passing by at a leisurely three knots, and small white-caps slapping the rocky shore.

"Lads!" roared a voice the other side of their door. "Get yourselves moving!"

Jake and Peter both dived for their shoes at the same time, bumping skulls in the process.

"This isn't exactly a first-class cabin," Jake joked, rubbing his head as he tied his shoes. "Wonder if Captain Tyrant has woken Valerie up too."

"Doubt it," Peter responded. "She's not a lad. And we may not be first-class passengers, but if we work like devils all morning, this afternoon is our dive time."

They opened their door and flew down the shoulder-width passageway to the dinette, where Gavin was sitting at the table clipping his fingernails. Dirty pots, pans, and plates were piled high on the counter in the galley behind him. He smoothed his hair as the boys entered. "Morning, lads. Captain and I left last night's dishes for you. The whole galley could use a scrubbing after you're done: top to bottom. If you pass inspection on that, there's heads to clean—that's toilets in boat language—the deck to mop, the brightwork to oil, the brass bell to rub down, and the oil to change in the engine room. I'll direct you on the last one."

"I know how to do that," Jake spoke up. He was proud his dad had taught him.

Gavin leveled a glare at him. "I said I'll supervise." His face rearranged itself into a forced smile. "Maybe Valerie will be up by then to keep you company." He finished his nails and dropped the clipper into his white shirt pocket with a flourish.

Jake felt the *Adrienne* shudder as someone cut the engine. Captain Dylan was in the cockpit above them dropping anchor. The loud splash was followed by the clink-clink of the chain running out of the boat.

"Guess the captain has arrived at a favorite fishing spot," Gavin commented, his eyes darting around the galley. Jake thought Gavin seemed suddenly nervous —but then, the man was often nervous.

"Oh," Gavin continued, "breakfast is whatever you find, depending on whether you want to add to that pile of dishes. There's no Chef François this weekend, poor us. But Miss Sheppard tells me Jake's not bad in a kitchen. So see what you can rustle up for the five of us for lunch, Jakey-Boy."

Jake didn't think much of that nickname. He watched Gavin rise, finger a shiny gold chain around his neck, and look directly at Peter.

"Not a minute of sloughing off, lads, or there'll be no diving this afternoon. I'm off to the library for a short meeting with Captain Dylan, now."

He'd hardly spoken the captain's name when the man himself ducked his head through the doorway. He stood in the galley, arms crossed, towering over his fellow boat mates, frowning and delivering the silent treatment to everyone present. Jake was amused to see

Gavin jump up from the table and begin rearranging the stack of pots and pans, as if he'd been caught playing on work time. Bet Captain Dylan doesn't waste time clipping his fingernails, Jake thought.

"You're up late, mates. Get a move on," the captain said in his baritone voice, nodding toward the sink. "Leave 'em, Gavin."

"I certainly was doing just that, sir. Trying to organize the boys, is all." He wiped his hands on a dishtowel and fingered his chain nervously.

"What's that?" Captain Dylan asked, stabbing a thick, calloused finger at Gavin's chest.

Gavin turned startled eyes to his boss, down to his chain, and to Captain Dylan's finger. "A chain," he said a little weakly.

"What's on it?" the captain pressed impatiently.

Gavin pulled the chain from inside his neatly ironed shirt to display a pressed square of copper. "An artifact reproduction from the gallery in Tofino that I purchased yesterday," he stated, eyes moving uncertainly to the captain's rock-hard face. "It imitates pre-contact copper," he offered in a quieter voice.

"I clearly pay you too much," Captain Dylan declared, then grunted, turned around, and exited as abruptly as he'd come. Gavin scurried after him without another word to the boys.

"Pre-contact copper?" Jake queried. "What the heck does that mean?"

Peter was opening one cupboard door after another in search of something to eat. "Pre-contact must mean it's a native thing, made before they had contact with white people."

"Oh," Jake said. His face brightened as he spotted a box on a high shelf. "Hey, Pop-Tarts! That's sure not something Chef François bought!"

The boys grabbed the box and loaded four of the pastries into the toaster, then yanked on the mini-fridge's door until it opened to reveal some orange juice. When they'd polished off yet another four Pop-Tarts, Jake set to work filling the sink with suds. Peter kept snooping in the cupboards for more food.

"What do you think they're meeting about?" Jake asked at length, suds up to his armpits.

Peter paused from shoveling handfuls of chocolate chips and raisins into his mouth from the baking cupboard. "Dunno. Navigation stuff? Best fishing places? Or maybe how to get us to do the 1,001 odd jobs they haven't had time for over the past two years."

Jake chuckled. "I'm afraid you've got that right. And hey, if you don't grab a towel and start drying these dishes, I'll interrupt those two to ask how to keelhaul you."

"Mmm-hmmm," Peter replied, his mouth too full of food to reply properly as he yanked a clean towel from a drawer and began flapping it around like he was a bullfighter.

An hour later, the two were on the deck with mops and buckets when the captain and first mate emerged from below decks dressed in "Tofino tuxedos": rain boots and raingear. Jake's eyes moved to the sky and saw that the gray clouds looked heavy with rain.

"We'll be back by lunchtime," the captain stated with no further explanation. "No messin' about."

Jake watched the two move down the companionway to the dinghy. Gavin untied the little boat and pulled the cord on its motor. Then they were off, accompanied only by the putt-putt of the motor and the cries of seagulls overhead. The boys watched them move through the gray water toward shore, then disappear around a rocky point without so much as a backward glance or wave.

"Only one fishing line between them," Peter remarked.

"Guess they're just scouting," Jake said. "Bet they took binoculars they'll turn on us every now and again, so we'd better keep working."

Jake noticed that Peter looked disappointed at this suggestion, but he put his mop into action again.

"Nice for Valerie that she's allowed to sleep in," Jake said after a while. He didn't really mind; he just wanted to see her.

"She's a paying customer," Peter reminded him.

Jake turned to peer at the headland point around

which the men had motored. His mop halted.

"Peter, do you see what I see?" He pointed to an animal out on the point, sniffing the fresh ocean air.

"A wolf," Peter exclaimed. Jake had never seen a wolf before. It looked like a large husky or a German shepherd dog, yet as it turned and loped away, the primal way it moved sent shivers down his spine.

"Totally wild," Peter said, shaking his head in amazement.

"Crazy," Jake agreed.

"Scary," a girl's voice added.

Jake and Peter swung around. Valerie looked stunning in a red blouse, black trousers, and velvet shoes, Jake decided. A touch of makeup made her fresh face glow.

"*Salut!*" Jake said.

"Good morning!" Peter enthused.

"What hard workers," she observed with a twinkle in her eyes. "This I think is Gavin's influence."

Influence would be one way to put it, Jake thought with an ironic grin. "Have you been up long?" he asked her casually.

"An hour. In my stateroom. The *Adrienne*'s library has big selection of books about this region."

"Really?" Peter asked, mop behind his back as if trying to hide it. "Even though there's not much around here?"

"Oh, there is much here," she said provocatively.

"Such as?" Jake asked.

"Ancient native villages with plank buildings and—how you say?—totem poles with forest growing around, and sunken ships from when Spaniards visit here in 1700s, and burial caves …"

"Burial caves?" Peter asked before Jake got a chance.

"Caves where natives placed deceased leaders with their most favorite possessions."

"And then the high tide would take it all away?" Jake suggested.

"No, in secret places above high-tide mark. The bodies would become mummified. Can you imagine finding such exciting place?" she asked as she scanned the shore to their right, then swiveled her head to study a nearby island, its cliffs soaring up into dark clouds. "Like discovering Egyptian pyramids. Some are the same age: 5,000 years old."

"But it would be disrespectful to touch that kind of stuff," Jake spoke up as the morning's first raindrops began to splatter. "Maybe even bad luck."

Valerie turned and surveyed Jake at length, making his face go very hot. "But why?" she asked coolly. "It belong in museum. No one is here now. No one care."

Jake knew there were still plenty of native communities in the area. He couldn't believe Valerie would ignore that fact. But he felt silenced by her dismissive look. He'd spent a lot of time last night thinking he'd detected some interest from her. He wasn't about to blow his big chance at encouraging their mutual attraction.

"So, what are you going to do this morning while we're finishing up our chores?" Peter asked eagerly.

"Oh, I have letters to write," Valerie said, turning a sunny smile on Peter. "Then I help you make lunch, if is okay."

"Absolutely," said Peter. "We'll do a gourmet lunch together, you and me."

Jake's teeth clenched. Peter couldn't cook a thing, and Jake's cooking abilities were well known around Sam's Adventure Tours. Hadn't Gavin specifically assigned lunch to Jake, not Peter? But Jake shrugged it off for the moment. Valerie would figure out soon enough who was practical and genuine, and who was all exaggeration and ego around here.

When she disappeared, silence reigned between the boys for a long time. The deck got the hardest scrubbing it had probably ever seen. Even after small talk began to creep back between them, the diligent labor and hint of tension remained. When their hands began blistering, Jake decided it was time to check out the engine room.

"You get to polish the woodwork and bell," he

ordered Peter. "I'm going to tackle the oil change."

"But Gavin said he had to be there for that."

Jake gave Peter a withering look. "I could change the oil on this boat in my sleep. I'm a mechanic's son, remember?" With that, he drew himself up and stalked down to the engine room.

As he opened the door and pulled the cord on the overhead light bulb, he felt the oppressive heat and stuffiness of the cramped crawlspace. He peeled off his sweater and breathed in the oily smell of the place. Working smells, his dad always called them. Jake smiled as he spotted a bucket, some fresh filters, and a crescent wrench. He crouched, then wriggled over to the drain valve. He paused, wondering if he should go against Gavin's orders, or surprise him with having all the chores finished by their return. *We can get diving sooner if we're all finished up by lunchtime,* he reasoned.

He scratched his head, then realized he still needed some rags. Finding none in the engine room, he went on a quick search up the passageway. He pulled open cupboard doors until he found one with neatly folded clothes on shelves. No rags here. Several Hawaiian shirts, some colorful bow ties. Oops. This was Gavin's cupboard. He was just about to close it when he spotted what looked like rags tossed on the cupboard's floor. He got down on his knees, plucked several good-sized rags from the pile and was about to shut the door again when a flash of bright metal winked out from among the rags. Clearing them away, he revealed a heavy brass box the size of a small suitcase. Even in the darkness of the cupboard, he could tell it was polished shinier than the ship's bell Peter was rubbing down right now.

Curious, Jake reached and tried to pull it out. It didn't want to budge. He shook his head, his imagination filling with stories of islands, pirates, and treasure chests. This box was clearly Gavin's pride. He shouldn't really sneak a peek, but … He glanced behind him to make sure no one was around, slowly eased the heavy box out, and lifted the lid.

Pieces of pounded, decorative copper—some resembling the square on Gavin's chain—caught the light filtering in along the passageway. Jake reached in and lifted out a copper bracelet. Beneath it nested some arrowheads and adzes—stone tools. The most attractive items in the box, however, were intricately woven baskets and a small wooden box with rounded edges.

Gavin really spent his wad in that gallery, Jake thought. And he sure likes reproductions of native artifacts.

Jake felt a bump against the side of the *Adrienne* and heard the captain chide Gavin. "Careful, you blundering idiot! And don't forget to fill 'er up before we go out again. She's near empty!"

As fast as he could, Jake closed up the brass box, shoved it back into the cupboard, and covered it with its camouflage of rags again. Heart beating fast, he closed the doors and hurried back to switch off the engine room light and shut that door. Then, slowing his steps, he made his way along the passageway. He had nearly reached the galley when the door swung open and Valerie emerged, looking elated.

"Come see what I make you," she said.

Beyond her was a tray of steaming soup bowls, fresh-baked bread, and a mountain of cookies on a serving plate. The aroma of her baking made his stomach growl.

"You—made—lunch," Jake stumbled.

"*Oui*, Jake, and if you will please to hit the dinner bell, I think Peter and the captain and first mate will arrive."

Jake grinned and called up to Peter to clang the ship's bell. This brought the captain and Peter at a quick gait, but Gavin seemed to have disappeared.

"I'll fetch Gavin," Jake offered, galloping down the passageway. When no one responded to his calls, he started to move aft. He jumped when he saw Gavin suddenly rise from his haunches in front of the very cupboard Jake had just closed moments before. Gavin looked just as startled, almost panicked. Then he produced a scowl worthy of the captain.

"What are you doing here, Jake? Thought you were fixing lunch."

"I'm looking for you to let you know lunch is on," Jake replied.

"Oh," Gavin said, throwing a quick glance at the cupboard floor before pushing the door shut. "Excellent."

Four hungry guys wolfed their lunch down as Valerie ate demurely, beaming at their praise. The captain and Gavin offered no commentary on their shore exploration, and the three teens refrained from asking.

"So, we can perhaps go diving soon?" Valerie asked Captain Dylan in her sweetest voice.

He coughed, laid down his soup spoon, and wiped his mouth awkwardly on the cloth napkin she'd laid on the table.

"Can't think why not, once Gavin has helped the boys change the oil, and I've pulled up to the island across the channel," he said gruffly. "Nancy and your parents have shown me your dive certificates. I'll expect you to go no deeper than thirty-five feet, use no more than forty-five minutes of air, and not go far from the boat. Agreed?"

Jake nodded.

"Agreed?" the captain bellowed, giving withering looks to Valerie and Peter, who had not bothered to respond. Their startled looks were quickly replaced by vigorous nodding.

"Okay. Gavin is a certified divemaster. He'll look over your equipment before you get into the water, and we'll expect you back here in an hour. We can come fetch you with the dinghy if you've drifted too far away to swim back."

He hesitated and drummed his fingers on the table for a minute. "Boys," he finally added, "Valerie has lots more dive time than you, so stick close to her, and do what she says."

Jake and Peter nodded obediently. Staying near Valerie's side was not a difficult assignment, Jake thought happily.

7   The Tunnel

Peter waited impatiently while the captain moved the *Adrienne* a few miles west of the coast. The tall man anchored the sloop along the eastern shore of a narrow island that rose so sharply in the middle Peter decided it resembled a shark's fin. He could hardly wait to get into the water. He hated the long process of pulling on his wetsuit, strapping the tank to his buoyancy vest, and pulling on the cursed weight belt. He hated defogging his face mask and checking everything, from the regulator through which he'd breathe, to the submersible pressure gauge. That was the awkward gadget that held his compass and informed him how much air he had.

He loved the "buddy check" part, however, because he'd volunteered to be Valerie's diving buddy and inspect her gear for her before Jake could. That Jake— he clearly had a little crush on the girl, but she was way out of his league. She was, in fact, just the girl Peter had been looking for. He'd swear off girl-watching entirely for her, honest.

Peter stood tall as he held up Valerie's buoyancy vest. She shrugged into it, buckled it up, and organized the bits and pieces that hung off it. Peter stepped back. Whoa, she looked good in diving gear. Too bad this wasn't the Bahamas, where she might dive in a bikini. Peter did a cursory check of Jake's equipment, then grinned his most flirtatious grin at Valerie as she inspected him. Serious diver that she was, of course, she stuck to the task at hand.

The three moved down to the swim grid, more than ready to jump in the water, swim fins and all. Who cared that it was cold and raining? This was fun time. The whole ocean floor awaited them.

Peter went first, surfacing with a "Yahoo!" The captain and Gavin didn't crack a smile the whole time they were seeing the three off. You'd think we were off to somewhere dangerous, Peter mused. He was totally psyched about doing his first dive without an instructor shadowing him. He turned face-down and peered through his face mask. Excellent visibility. Already, he could see passing rockfish, their tail fins wagging busily. He lifted his face, winked at Valerie, and pointed to the island beside them.

"Shall we swim along the wall here for a while and look for anemones?"

"*Oui*," Val responded. "Let's use our snorkels and save air." She waited until Jake nodded his head in agreement.

Kicking slowly to conserve energy, the three divers let their swim fins take them up alongside the island. A gentle current moved along the wall of rock. The tide was halfway between low and high, and rising, Peter noticed. Brightly colored sea stars and sea cucumbers crowded in the intertidal zone, allowing the divers to float along like browsers in an art gallery, still breathing through their snorkels as they stayed on the water's surface.

After almost fifteen minutes of drifting, they decided to see what was deeper. They formed a small huddle, deflated their buoyancy vests together, and switched from snorkel to regulator. Then they sank, smiling at one another through their masks and practicing some of the hand signals they'd learned during dive training.

It always took a minute to get used to the loud whooshing of his own breathing through his regulator, but Peter's excitement grew as the island's lower wall began to reveal ever-greater bursts of color and marine-life variety. He wanted to reach out and touch the purple sea urchins and cactus-shaped glassy sea squirts, but he knew this was neither safe nor respectful of the marine life.

Sticking close together, the three continued to both

descend and move south along the wall, leaving a trail of bubbles above. The boys let Valerie lead. She was quick to point her gloved fingers at interesting life, and Peter liked the leisurely pace she set. No point hurrying when the current itself was making the travel easy. After ten minutes, he sensed—and his compass confirmed—that they were rounding the southern point of the island, but no one made any move to surface. They hugged the island's western shore now and moved slowly north. If they had any difficulty swimming back, the men would come fetch them here in the dinghy. Perhaps Gavin and the captain had already watched their bubble trail round the point through binoculars.

As they hung weightless over the bottom, Peter caught sight of a curled-up giant Pacific octopus. He tapped Valerie on the shoulder, pointed to it, and saw her face light up. He wished he had an underwater camera: to capture the thrill on her beautiful face, not the octopus. He counted eight arms on the pale red, globular body. What had Nancy told him? That this was the largest species of octopus in the world? Sometimes the tentacles were more than five feet long. Very tasty, too.

Valerie checked her compass and depth gauge—they were still at thirty-five feet—and signaled for each of them to check their air supply. Through sign language, they each reported that they had used only about one-third of their air supply: fifteen minutes' worth. Even so, she jabbed her finger upward. Obediently, the boys followed her slowly to the surface—knowing that if they rose too fast, they wouldn't decompress sufficiently, and that could cause health problems.

"That current was strong," Valerie observed as the three surfaced. "We're around the corner of the island, which means the *Adrienne* can't see us, but captain and first mate are just few minutes away by dinghy, so I think we are fine. Look! Another island!"

Jake and Peter spun to observe a flatter island to the west, one that had been hidden from view by the steep island they'd just rounded. As Peter was judging the new island to be close enough to swim to, a mighty splash between the two islands made their jaws loosen.

"Check it out! Dolphins!" Peter shouted. He could hardly believe his eyes. A pod of more than twenty-five Pacific white-sided dolphins was breaching and playing, their sleek black backs complemented by white bellies. Like a parade of joyful partygoers, they leaped and arched in mid-air before hitting the ocean, leaving an impressive rooster tail of water.

"I've heard of swimmers and divers traveling with schools of them," said Jake. "They're the friendliest of the dolphin family."

"They're moving so fast." Valerie's gaze followed the dolphins, her eyes wide.

"This is a chance of a lifetime!" As he struck out toward the school, Peter heard the ever-cautious Jake protesting, "But …"

Peter didn't care. With one backward glance, he saw that Valerie, too, wasn't going to let this opportunity pass. She was a gutsy, decisive girl, a little on the strong-willed side. Just the way he liked 'em. Jake was soon trailing them. Again, they stayed on the surface and breathed through their snorkels to save their tank air.

Though he felt encumbered by the thick wetsuit, weights, and tank on his back, Peter was strong and made it across the channel in record time. The dolphins seemed unfazed and allowed him to get up close. He turned to grin at his two mates, then switched to his regulator and sank to watch the show underwater. Such noise! Such bubbles! Such grace in the fast-moving creatures. This was truly a sight he'd never forget his entire life. Like Valerie and Jake, he tried swimming alongside the graceful creatures, but it was like butting a bicycle onto a race-car track. So he settled for floating alongside until the long lineup had passed. The last dolphin winked at him, he was sure.

When they surfaced, the three were breathless with excitement. They were also close to the second island's eastern shore.

"I nearly touched one," Valerie enthused.

"Couldn't believe how big they were close-up," Jake exclaimed. "Did you see the baby? She was nearly as long as I am tall."

"*Très jolie*," Valerie agreed. "Let us do one last dive along the shore here. Then we must head back."

Peter nodded. "We're good for about another thirty minutes under water. Then we can swim back with snorkels, or wait here for the dinghy."

The three nodded and let themselves sink together. Peter was careful to keep both his mates within sight, which wasn't difficult, given the spectacular visibility in this region. At thirty feet, they began moving along the rock wall, this time sighting abalone, an orange-and-white speckled sea slug, and sunflower stars.

Within minutes, Peter came across the entrance to a cave. He moved into the darkness, scanning the wall for little cavities where interesting fish might be hiding. He checked behind him to make sure Valerie and Jake were following, then pulled out his flashlight. There! He trained the light on a fist-sized opening in the wall of the cave. "Anyone home?" he voiced silently.

In reply, the profoundly ugly face of a wolf eel greeted him. Peter backed up, then began laughing, sending a cascade of bubbles to the ceiling of the sculpted cavern. He pointed wildly at his find and his companions moved in closer for a look. The wolf eel continued to glare at them. Its gray, puckered scowl seemed consistent with its warty, misshapen body and bulging eyes. When its mate poked her head out, too, Peter gripped Valerie's shoulders to make sure she saw. Valerie cocked her head as if saying hello to it.

What had Nancy told them about wolf eels? Some are longer than human beings. They have strong, crushing jaws with thick, spiky teeth, and brave divers can feed them. Peter had no treats on him, but he was so buoyed by his discovery that he decided to move deeper into the cave, flashlight leading the way.

Valerie soon caught up and tapped him on his shoulder, then pointed to their gauges. Peter signaled back the number on his pressure gauge. Twelve minutes left. He knew that was getting low, but it was still pretty safe. The others reported similar amounts of air. Taking the lead now, Peter decided to explore just a little farther. That's when he saw a beam of light ahead. So this wasn't a cave. It was a tunnel. A very wide tunnel. Maybe a tunnel leading to the open ocean on the other side of the island. How cool would that be? He moved forward. The others followed.

All along the tunnel he could see crabs and shrimp, though not much more. Perhaps because very little life could thrive in this semi-darkness. Swimming for that light was turning out to be a chore. He was tired and beginning to feel a little chilly. They'd been in the water for just over an hour, and no doubt the captain and first mate were starting up the dinghy motor at this very moment.

Peter felt a tug on his swim fin. Valerie had caught up to him and was signaling a suggestion to turn around and return the way they'd come. He pointed to the light up ahead. She hesitated, as if tempted, then pointed to her gauge. Ten minutes left. Ten minutes, Peter considered. Down to the wire, for sure, but he knew that where there was light, there was air, and there was lots of light ahead. You're not supposed to run your air down to zero—it's bad for the tanks as well as dangerous—but that broad swath of light had a hold on him.

Jake pulled up, frowning, and signaled that he wanted to turn around. That was enough to convince Valerie.

He was outnumbered. Peter nodded and turned with them. As he began swimming, however, he saw why Jake was worried. The tidal flow was against them. They were going to have to use lots of muscle to swim against this current before their air ran out. Peter felt a bolt of panic. Why hadn't he tuned into the fact that they were being pushed gently down the tunnel by a current? They were all strong, but they were also tired, and he could tell from the way both Valerie and Jake were kicking that they were scared now, too. He tugged on one of Valerie's swim fins, gave her the "low air" signal, and pointed back to the light. He knew she understood, but she hesitated. Which way was safer now? They'd wasted precious time trying to double back, and the current was getting stronger. Getting to a place they could surface before they ran too low was now the number one goal.

Peter watched Valerie's strong leg muscles catch up to Jake and tug on his swim fin. She motioned for him to turn around and toward the bright light. Jake's eyes grew wide, he shook his head no, and looked to Peter. Peter pointed toward the light in a grave manner, to show him that, like Valerie, he'd weighed the options carefully.

Peter didn't like the look in Jake's eyes, but every second they hesitated, the tide was pushing them farther into the tunnel. So the three turned toward the light, Valerie leading, and began kicking for their lives. The light grew brighter, but their air supply was diminishing. Fear and vigorous swimming uses up air faster than anything, Peter remembered. He tried to calm himself, the way he'd learned during training. Breathe—slowly. Breathe—slowly.

When Jake's hand closed around his ankle, he turned around, fearful that Jake had run out of air. He was right. Jake's frantic hand signal was a slash across the throat. Valerie saw it too, but Peter acted so fast Valerie barely had time to move toward them. Peter nodded and pulled in close to Jake, allowing Jake to grab Peter's second regulator—the one a diving buddy is supposed to use in just such an emergency. Every diver's tank runs lines to two regulators, just in case. Jake took one last gasp on his own disappearing air, tore his regulator out of his mouth, and exhaled slowly into the water as he prepared to fit Peter's spare into his mouth. His eyes were wide, but he wasn't panicking, yet.

Peter had to fight his own inclination to hold his breath until Jake had successfully switched to breathing from Peter's air supply. They locked arms exactly the way they'd learned in training, to keep the short line between Peter's tank and Jake's mouth from pulling out. In all the sessions the two had practiced this, never had it occurred to Peter that they'd actually have to use it. Now the question was, how long would Peter's tank hold out with two divers depleting its meager supply?

The tunnel no longer seemed wide; both boys' shoulders were brushing its edges as they swam locked together. Valerie was nodding encouragement at them and sticking close. Peter knew that she knew the score. Should the boys run out, they would have to do buddy breathing on her spare regulator: one inhaling on it while the other exhaled into the water, handing it back and forth. That would be tricky, maybe even impossible in this tunnel. Three divers breathing from one tank and two regulators wasn't something Peter wanted to experience next.

Suddenly the light was above instead of ahead of them. They headed up, all three holding hands and kicking slowly to ensure a safe ascent. As they burst to the surface, the overwhelming relief of being able to drop the regulators from their mouths and breathe fresh air was instantly slammed by a dark realization of where they were.

8   Escape

Jake was still gasping, more from fright than lack of air. He'd tried not to breathe faster than normal as they'd moved through the tunnel, but the fear of drowning by inhaling water can bring on hyperventilation, which can empty a tank fast. He felt overwhelmed with thankfulness that Peter had been there for him, that they'd changed to the alternative breathing system as smoothly as they had during their certification exam.

But with one crisis over, all he could do was gape, shivering, at the giant domed cave now holding them prisoner. Light flooded in from the large hole in its domed ceiling. Like a skylight, or a whale's blowhole if I were in the whale's belly, Jake thought ruefully. Or maybe like being inside a hollow volcano, looking up through its neck.

Raindrops floated down from the hole and stung

his upturned face. Something hung down from it. His face mask was fogged and he didn't feel he had the strength to tear it off his face. Probably a vine.

He shivered as the desperation of their situation sank in. They'd been immersed in fifty-five-degree Fahrenheit seawater for one and a half hours now. Divers in wetsuits usually feel the chill set in around this time. Fine motor skills—the ability to use one's hands—begin to deteriorate after about two hours, which is why surfers sometimes need help unzipping their wetsuits when they come out of the water. Hypothermia, Jake knew from guide training, can start to set in any time after that, along with impaired judgment and, eventually, unconsciousness. The process speeds up when a diver stops generating heat through movement.

Jake ripped off his mask with a trembling hand and thought through their options. They no longer had enough air to swim out the tunnel no matter what direction the current flowed. And judging from the barnacles on the sides of this cave, high tide would never lift them high enough to crawl out the blow-hole. Captain Dylan and Gavin would search both the steep island and this one—were probably hunting desperately for them right now—but the chances of them looking down a trapdoor-sized hole in what would resemble a pile of rocks from above was a long shot. His stomach tightened. He pushed a fist into the wall, forcing himself to breathe slowly to stem the rising panic and anger.

Jake studied the walls of the dome. Ledges stuck out far enough that they could crawl onto them, but what good would that do? With nothing but wetsuits on, they'd succumb to the cold eventually. He looked for a shelf large enough for all three and identified several. If they huddled tightly together, it would slow down the deadly chill, but in the end, hypothermia was sure to take them, probably before the next low tide. They were destined to be fish food before the next morning's light. He wrapped his arms around his chest.

He looked at Valerie's widened eyes and Peter's furrowed brow. We should have fought that current with everything we had, Jake thought, instead of trusting a beam of light to give us false hope. The truth is, we should never have wandered past the wolf eels in the first place. But like Valerie and Peter, he hadn't sensed the current until it was too late. None of us are really to blame. He shivered again.

"Okay, guys," Peter spoke as he released his weight belt and heaved it up onto a shelf. "I think we need to ditch our tanks and weights, climb up as high as we can on the shelves, and wait for high tide to reach that rope."

Rope? Jake squinted above him. Sure enough, it was a rope, not a vine. The end of it dangled three to four feet above them, but that's a long way when one has to wait for a tide to travel that far. And even if they could pull themselves up on ledges before then, they'd have to struggle to lean out far enough to grab it.

"Someone must live on this island," Valerie speculated, brightening. "This must be swimming place at high tide. Why else a rope?"

"There's probably a vacation cabin," Peter corrected her. "And if some kids decided to make this their swimming hole, it sure wouldn't be with their parents' knowledge. It's too dangerous. But if high tide takes us up to that rope, we've got a way out."

"Hey, at high tide this might make a cool little swimming place," Jake suggested. "There's no wind or waves in here, and the water's no colder than the ocean."

"No warmer, either," Valerie inserted as she clenched her teeth together to keep them from chattering. She swam to the nearest ledge, unbuckled her weight belt, and slid it up onto the rock. Next, she tore her mask off her face and slipped it over the weight belt, securing it there with the belt buckle. Then she shed her buoyancy vest and expertly released her tank from it, shoving the heavy metal cylinder up beside the belt. She kept her diving knife and flashlight.

Jake's brain flashed him an image of archaeologists finding their weight belts, masks, and tanks still sitting on these shelves in fifty years, perhaps with the three divers' skeletons rattling around them in the water. His skin prickled and his mouth went very dry.

Valerie turned to look at Jake as she pulled her buoyancy vest back on. "These give a little warmth," she said as she watched Jake and Peter finish shedding their equipment, re-don their vests, and hoist themselves up on a large ledge. She swam over to join them. Now the water came only to their calves as their legs dangled over the shelf's edge. They bent to remove their swim fins.

"If we stay out of the water, we slow down heat loss," she stated like a diving instructor addressing vacationing students from a sunny dock. "I think high tide maybe come in one hour."

Three pairs of eyes rose to the rope and wondered. How cold would they be in an hour? Would the water touch the bottom of the rope by then? Would the rope hold them? Would they each have the strength to climb up it? Jake had another question nagging at him. How would Peter's fear of heights—something Valerie didn't know about—affect Peter's climbing attempt?

Jake had always excelled at climbing the big rope in his school gym. But doing hand-over-hand holds on a professionally knotted rope situated above a gym mat was not going to be the same as climbing an ancient polypropylene rope whose surface anchor was a mystery. Jake took a sideways glance at Valerie. She was strong and determined for a girl, but he'd never known a girl at his school to make it very far up the rope in the gym. Girls weren't made for that. He and Peter might have to pull her up from the top, not an easy task even if she was small and lightweight.

For fifteen minutes, the three sat on the ledge, speaking little.

"Hey, this sofa isn't very comfortable," Peter joked after a while. "And where's the big-screen television and popcorn?"

Valerie giggled. Jake cracked a smile. Peter was always good at coaxing a laugh out of people, no matter how grim their circumstances. Jake, his throat parched, stuck his tongue out to catch some raindrops falling from the hole in the dome high above them. Tiny as the droplets were, they tasted good. He lifted one of his swim fins and held it to catch a little more, then fed the micro stream of rainwater down his gullet. Soon all three were attempting the same. It gave them something to do, even if it failed to quench their building thirst.

Soon saltwater lapped at their knees and crept coldly into their laps. "It's time," Jake pronounced, and the three slipped reluctantly into the water and swam to a higher ledge, clutching only their swim fins, as if in silent agreement that fins might still be of some use if they escaped this cave.

"If some kids adopted this as their secret swimming place, they should have drilled some hooks in the wall and hung waterproof containers of food just above the tide line," Peter joked when they were settled on the next shelf.

"And towels and blankets," Jake added. He was shivering so hard his words came out like a stutter. He shot a look at his companions. Peter was shivering, but less so. Valerie had tucked herself into a ball and seemed to be doing okay. Jake wished he had more body fat. It's body fat that was going to determine who held up best over the forty-five minutes till high tide, he reflected. Hypothermia, or a serious core-body temperature drop, would begin to threaten their judgment and eventually their lives.

Fifteen minutes and two ledge-changes later, their watery elevator had lifted them much closer to the rope, but it was not yet within reach. This was a grim race, Jake reflected. Their body heat was slowly flowing out of them as the tide was flowing into the cave. Which would win? Jake was shaking almost uncontrollably now. He saw Valerie studying him. She moved toward him and asked him to unfurl his gloved hands. "Can you open and close hands?" she asked with concern.

Jake did so, slowly but successfully. "Huddle," she declared solemnly. The three wrapped their arms around one another with no hesitation or embarrassment. This wasn't about romance; it was about survival, Jake knew. Nature has a way of making priorities very clear at times. Any other day, Jake would have welcomed Valerie's embrace as proof that they were meant to be together. But his half-numbed mind and shaking body had no room for such thoughts at the moment.

At long last, the maddeningly slow tide influx brought them within reach of the rope. Jake was the first to stand up on their ledge. Peter was as tall as him, but made no move to go first. Jake knew that Peter's fear of heights was why.

"I'm going first," Jake declared, to nods all around. He flexed his still-gloved hands, but before applying them to the thick nylon rope, he held them out for his companions to slap.

"You can do it, old buddy," Peter said.

"Good luck," Valerie said softly, squeezing his hand for a moment.

Jake looked up. Thirty feet to the hole, he guessed. No higher than the rope in the gym. He pictured his athletic gym teacher, Mr. Pappajohn, standing on the mat, shouting encouragement. He pictured a huddle of schoolmates cheering him on. He wrapped his palms around the first knot and pulled himself up, lifted an arm, did it again. Halfway up, he felt his limbs trembling. For a moment, he feared he was going to drop back into the cold water. He clenched his fists tighter, glued his eyes on the hole, and lifted his feet to a large knot. Then, pushing hard against it, he shimmied up a little higher, clenching his chattering jaw, aiming for that hole.

If nothing else, the exertion was warming him a little. And the relief that flooded him when he was finally able to lift a knee onto the wet rock of the hole's rim took his breath away. He scrambled up onto his feet. It wasn't a big island, maybe three blocks tip-to-tip, and much narrower than it was long. Rain still floated down. He felt no warmer for being out of the cave, and he knew the threat of hypothermia remained. He inspected the tree on which the rope was anchored and scanned the island for any signs of the captain and Gavin. He even sprinted a short distance on shaky legs up to a higher viewpoint, to see if he could spot their dinghy in the water.

Nothing but lapping ocean and salal—the West Coast's ever-present scrub brush. Though disappointment gnawed, he knew there was no time to lose getting his mates up.

He lay on his stomach and peered down as Peter tried to help Valerie climb the rope. As Jake had guessed, strong as she was, she couldn't pull her entire body up with an arm hold.

"Peter, you come up next, and if we need to, we can pull Valerie up together," he ordered. Peter nodded, and Valerie lowered herself back to the shelf, looking defeated.

Peter lifted his hands high on the rope and pulled himself up easily. But his face was pressed against the rope, and his eyes were darting everywhere.

"Easy, Peter, just breathe slowly. Close your eyes," Jake coached.

Peter's eyes closed tight. His hands fumbled for the next hold. Jake could see Peter's powerful upper body muscles rippling through his wetsuit. Halfway up, he opened his eyes.

"Don't look down," Jake ordered, but it was too late. One glance, then a momentary loosening of his grip, and he fell backwards, plunging into the water.

9   The Island

J ake watched Valerie's arm come up instinctively to protect her from the tremendous splash. Then she leaned out and helped Peter back on the shelf. As she had with Jake, she held his hands tightly until his shivering abated. "You can do it, Peter. I know you can."

This time Peter wouldn't look at Jake. He must be feeling humiliated, and surely his confidence has been shattered, Jake thought. "You were nearly there, Peter. That means you can do it," Jake called down.

This time, Peter's face revealed fury. He reached up aggressively, pulled himself high, and repeated the move. His eyes locked on Jake's face, occasionally shifting to a knot he was trying to reach. Fueled by anger and determination, he pulled his dripping body upward in neat lunges, until Jake locked his arms under Peter's armpits and helped draw him up the rest of the way.

"Thanks," Peter mumbled, shaking as he curled up on a rock for a second.

"No biggie," Jake said, slapping him on his shoulder. "I kind of owed you for those puffs of air."

They crawled back to the hole and looked down. To their surprise, they found Valerie busy tying three pairs of swim fins onto the bottom of the rope. "Pull, garçons," she shouted up, smiling.

"Good thinking," Peter said in amazement. "French surfer girls have their wits about them, don't they, Jake?"

So they'd saved the fins, but Jake wondered if the tanks and weight belts, now well covered by water on shelves far below, would ever be retrieved. At least they knew where they were and had done their best not to lose the expensive equipment. He and Peter pulled on the rope till the swim fins were in their hands, then dropped it back to Valerie. Now Jake moved to the big tree around which the rope was anchored and pulled out his diving knife.

"Cedar," he declared to Peter.

"Huh?" Peter asked. "Have you forgotten about Valerie?"

"Not at all," Jake said.

Peter looked down at Valerie, and back at Jake. "Just a minute, Val," he called. He watched Jake lean down and make a horizontal slash with his knife on the lower tree, then begin peeling a strip of bark up from the cut.

"What the heck?" Peter asked. "You're ruining this tree."

"Actually," Jake said, "I've heard that the Nuu-chah-nulth natives around here know how to take enough inner bark for baskets and still let the tree live." He lifted his strip of bark to the ground and sliced it into three neat ribbons, discarding the outer bark as he reached for the less brittle inner bark. "Now help me braid these," he ordered, not bothering to explain.

Peter shrugged and held the strands at one end. Jake twisted as fast as his stiff hands would let him. As they completed the task and were carrying the braid to the hole, they heard Valerie exclaim "Oh!"

The two looked over the edge of the opening.

Valerie was smiling, but her hand was over her mouth. A seal's head had popped up near her and was observing her silently. It disappeared as fast as it had emerged.

"Better than visit from shark," Valerie tried to joke.

"There are sharks around here, but they've never been a problem," Jake reassured her. "And even in areas they're supposedly a problem, it's totally exaggerated."

"Mmmm," Valerie responded, scanning the water around her as she shivered. "Why so long up there?"

Jake smiled, hauled up the rope, and tied his cedar braid securely to its bottom. He handed the other end of the braid to Peter and motioned for him to stand on the other side of the hole.

"Valerie," he said, "we're lowering you down a swing. Sit in the loop and hold on to the sides very tightly."

"*Quoi?*" she asked.

"*Une balançoire,*" he repeated.

Her upturned face gawked at the "U" of extended rope coming her way. But she seated herself primly, like a small child at a park swing-set, and gripped the sides for dear life.

"Ready, set, pull," Jake ordered, and he and Peter hauled their respective ropes hand-over-hand, like tug-o-war contestants. It was hard work, especially with hands that no longer seemed to do as they ordered them, and with slippery rock underfoot. But Jake knew it was the only way. They'd never have been able to pull Valerie up on a straight rope, not even two strong guys against a petite girl. Resting once or twice, but never losing their grip on the rope, the two eventually maneuvered her up. All three gave each other a quick embrace.

"*Merci beaucoup,*" she said, hanging her head. "I'm not so good for climbing."

"Now what?" Peter asked.

"There has to be a cabin on this island," Jake ruled, face grim. "And it had better be close." The three broke into a slow jog, their wetsuit booties squishing against the hemlock needles, their still-gloved hands stuffed into their swim fins to help them push salal branches away from them. Moving helped put some circulation back into his body, but Jake felt seriously cold, as if nothing but a hot tub and down parka could reverse the heat loss. He pictured a hot, steaming bathtub in a cabin not far away; it kept him moving through the wet, tangled brush.

He stumbled several times and was helped to his feet by his companions. When he heard Peter shout, he broke into the best run that hobbled legs could muster. Sure enough, a tiny log cabin with an ocean view to the west sat in a clearing. Peter grabbed for the door handle, turned it to no avail, and shook it in dismay. "It's locked!"

"Of course it's locked," Jake said. "And it's wrong to break in. Except that any owner would understand this was an emergency." He circled the cabin, found no other door, and returned to the simple structure's only window. Peter helped him jimmy open the window, then climbed inside to open the door for his mates.

The three searched closets and cupboards in the cramped kitchen and bedroom as if on a mission. There was no bathroom, let alone a bathtub full of steaming water, which meant there must be an outhouse nearby. But a pile of quilts stored in a zippered plastic holder and tucked into a dusty cupboard was good enough for Jake. He felt badly about disturbing private property, but this was urgent. If they didn't get warm soon, they were in serious trouble. As Valerie searched the bedroom, he tore off his wetsuit without an ounce of modesty, wrapped two quilts around himself, and threw the rest at Peter.

Valerie emerged from the bedroom in an oversized pink nightgown and a pair of boys' shorts just her size, complete with suspenders. She tucked the nightie into her shorts and posed for them with a cartoon-imprinted bath towel hugging her shoulders like a shawl.

"What do you think?" she joked tiredly.

"I think you need some fashion advice from Gavin," Peter responded, face sliding into a big grin. "Are there more clothes in there?" His wetsuit was half off.

"Yes," she replied.

Jake and Peter slipped into the bedroom, slammed the door, and minutes later paraded out in rolled-up men's jeans and men's undershirts. Paint-splotched sweatshirts hung in their hands, but were on them in a jiffy. Jake felt much better already, but also very tired.

Peter walked to the kitchen taps and turned them. Not a drop came out.

"I think owners not come here often," Valerie observed, running a finger through a giant cobweb and writing her initials in some dust. "And no telephone or radio."

Peter exited the cabin and returned with a plastic

bowl of fresh rainwater. The three sipped greedily from it, brushing away the hemlock needles that stuck to their lips. When they'd drunk their fill, the three lowered themselves into faded, slightly musty armchairs and looked at one another.

Peter's face turned serious and he looked at his watch. "It'll be dark in three hours. We should be down on the beach looking for the dinghy, and maybe figuring out where we are exactly. They have to be searching for us. If we don't see them, we'll try to build a fire so they'll see our smoke."

Jake eased himself further into his chair. He knew Peter was right, but he felt capable of nothing but falling asleep. Traipsing around in the rain without raingear after he'd only just begun to warm up didn't entice him one bit.

"I will go," Valerie offered.

"That's great, Valerie. Jake, you stay here and rest. Two of us is enough," Peter declared gallantly with a hint of an agenda that irritated Jake, but not enough to make him rise from the worn chair on which he was curled up.

"Okay," Jake murmured. A third person wouldn't really make a difference, he told himself. But he felt a little guilty as he moved to the bedroom and lay down on one of the two single beds there. He heard the kitchen door slam as Peter and Valerie left. He looked around him. A folding bed was pushed up near the foot of the other beds—for the boy who'd strung the rope down into the cave, Jake guessed. Jake rested his head on a musty pillow and fell asleep so fast that the rain pounding at the window might as well have been soundless.

Scuffling in the next room brought him slowly back to consciousness. In his dream, he was ascending gently from the ocean's stony floor in a shower of light-filled bubbles. When he opened his eyes, the darkness was thick, impenetrable. Where am I? "Hey! What's going on?" he mumbled.

"Did I wake you?" Peter whispered from the kitchen. His diving flashlight flicked on. Jake blinked. As Peter moved into the bedroom, memories of the day came flooding back.

"Did you find the captain and Gavin?" said Jake, trying to shake off his heavy sleep.

"No," came the solemn answer.

"And the *Adrienne*?"

"No sign of it or the dinghy when we searched before dark. But if it's still where it was anchored, that tall island between us is keeping it out of sight. We have a signal fire going down on the beach. Valerie is tending it. Maybe you can take over when you're ready."

"Sure," Jake said, springing up. "You must be exhausted, Peter. Sorry I jammed out on you earlier, but I'm good now." Not good for much, really, but definitely better.

He let Valerie off duty and, wrapped in quilts, dozed off and on by the signal fire, thankful the rain had stopped. At first light, he leapt up, decided the fire was safe on its own for a while, and ran up and down the island. He circled it three times, breath coming in gasps, hemlock needles crunching underfoot. No dinghy. No yacht. Where were the helicopters and airplanes that the captain surely must have called in?

When he stepped into the cabin, Valerie was pouring a bowl of rainwater into a saucepan on the cramped kitchen's two-burner propane stove.

"No captain? No planes?" she asked.

"None," he replied.

She fired up the stove, then reached up and began opening kitchen cupboards. "Eeeuuwww, how do you say in English, Jake, *crottes de souris?*"

"Mouse turds," Jake responded, stomach cramping with hunger at the sound of the cupboard doors. "Anything more edible than that?"

"Soap, toilet paper, coffee and hot chocolate powder, rice, and two cans baked beans. Baked beans are very American, *oui?*"

"Canadian too," Peter offered as he emerged from

the bedroom with a yawn. "Don't tell me you're going to get fussy when we haven't eaten since yesterday noon?"

"But of course not. I make you some gourmet baked beans for breakfast, perhaps not with mouse turds for flavor. We will replace all food after we are rescued."

"I take it there's no sign of anyone looking for us?" Peter addressed Jake.

Jake nodded. "We'd better eat fast and get back down to the beach."

Sunshine crept into the kitchen as the three forked beans into their mouths.

"If they searched this island while we were in the cave, and searched the water around the two islands before that, they'd have assumed by now we're drowned," Jake pondered aloud. "But they'd surely have alerted the Coast Guard either way, which would have sent planes and helicopters and boats this way long before now. And the captain and Gavin would be doing more searches of the islands this morning."

The other two nodded soberly.

"Unless something happen to the captain and Gavin," Valerie offered softly.

"What could possibly happen to them?" Peter shot back. "Sorry, I didn't mean to say it like that."

"If for any reason they not contact the Coast

Guard, then Nancy and my parents not know anything wrong," Valerie continued, twisting her fork around and around in her hand.

"It's true that we're not expected back until tomorrow, but the captain and Gavin would never give up on us so easily, and they would alert authorities," Jake insisted.

"So we need to swim across the channel and walk around the tall island to shout at the *Adrienne*," Peter said. "Maybe we should have done that last night before dark."

"Nah. We were too cold and too tired. It may not be far, but we know how strong those currents are. Today we're rested and stronger," Jake said.

After breakfast, the three traipsed down to the beach and fed their signal fire some more green branches to create smoke. Jake appreciated the sun's warming rays as he crouched and held his hands toward the fire. Given yesterday's experience, he couldn't take warmth for granted. It's August, he reflected. Why shouldn't the sun feel warm?

As they set off along a path, his damp wetsuit booties—the only footwear option available—felt clammy but protected his feet from the uneven ground. To their right, they kept looking out to the lapping Pacific Ocean. The water stretched west as far as Jake could see, all the way to Siberia, he figured.

There was no sign of a boat near or far.

"Let's try the other side," Peter suggested. They kept walking, circumnavigating their entire piece of real estate for the umpteenth time. As they came to the island's eastern side, they paused to study the tall island between them and the coast.

"Can you believe we were swimming with a pod of dolphins here just yesterday?" Peter mused.

"Took only about fifteen minutes to swim it," Valerie observed.

"The *Adrienne* is anchored just the other side," Peter insisted. "Even if there's a problem, we can swim back here. But let's wait for the tide to be just past slack, to be safest."

"Wonder how long they searched for us yesterday," Jake said. He hated to think of the men concluding that the three had drowned and radioing that information to Nancy. She'd surely been through enough agonizing close calls with Jake and Peter.

He spotted some red huckleberries and shoved a few into his mouth.

"Tart, but tasty," he informed the others. All three began pulling berries from the bushes, lifting their heads now and again to look out at the water, hoping for a sight of the dinghy or yacht.

Finally, they headed back to the cabin along the western beach, where branches of stunted Sitka spruce trees stuck out at odd angles, as if they had to elbow through high winds on a regular basis to stay alive.

Bet this place gets some sick surf waves, Jake thought.

"I stay here and watch for a while," Valerie announced.

"Sounds good," Peter said. "I'm going to do another search around the cabin. Jake, want to check the fire?"

Jake nodded and headed down the beach toward the wisp of smoke.

"Hi, Jake!" Valerie greeted him a short while later with a smile that made his heart do a flip-flop as she hurried toward him. "Look what I find!" She lifted a polished-looking oyster shell from her shorts pocket and held it out to him with sparkling eyes and a toss of her long, loose hair.

"Nice," he said, though he'd seen hundreds of them before. He was thinking how nice her sunlit hair looked blowing in the morning breeze.

"And this," she said, pulling one hand from behind her back and thrusting a tennis shoe at him.

"Uh-huh," he said, wishing she'd surprise him more by throwing her arms around him and hugging him for yesterday's rescue. "Doesn't look like it has ever been worn. Wonder if it's from that cargo of shoes dumped off Alaska."

"What cargo of shoes?" Valerie asked.

"A ship off southeast Alaska accidentally lost about 60,000 tennis shoes in the early '90s. About nine months later, so many washed up along the beaches in British Columbia, Washington, and Oregon, that people held swap meets to help them find a pair."

"So funny. This was, I think, before e-Bay."

Jake smiled. "Then, a few years after the spill, a bunch of them washed up in Hawaii, and a few years after that, in the Philippines and Japan. Can't remember when they were due in eastern North America, and at some point, they're expected back here."

"Except for the ones that are giving some poor whales stomach ache."

Jake laughed. He loved her quick sense of humor.

"I have another find," she said, hesitating for effect, her eyes mischievous.

"Yes?" he said, daring to move a little closer.

With a flourish, she pulled a copper bracelet turned green with age out of her shorts pocket and cradled it in her hands, lifting it to his face.

Jake looked at it curiously. It reminded him of a bracelet he'd seen in the brass box hidden in Gavin's stateroom. He'd almost forgotten about that box and hadn't yet mentioned it to anyone. He reached out to touch the bracelet in Valerie's hand, ran his fingers along its surface. It looked like it had been artistically pounded, but its age and condition made it impossible to see the designs without a good cleaning. It was very wide.

"Where did you find that?" he asked.

"On the beach. Showing little bit in the sand."

"Wow, that's quite a find. A native artifact, maybe."

"Yes, I also think this," she said, holding it up higher and looking up at him with such a pleased look that he almost took it as an invitation to kiss her. "I am excited to show to *Maman et Papa*." She smiled and then the light went out of her face. "They must be so worried if captain contacts them. What must they think? I wish they could know we are here on this island, safe."

"I don't think they're worrying because no one has reported us missing yet," Jake said, staring at the ground. "If they knew to worry, there'd be a search party out for us." He wasn't sure if that was comforting or not.

Valerie nodded, and her eyes returned to the bracelet. "It is worth very much money, yes?"

Jake frowned. "But if it's a native artifact, it's not yours to take," he said earnestly. "You need to give it to one of the local native band offices."

The warmth drained from Valerie's face as she clapped the bracelet on her arm and gave Jake a strange look. "Oh, yes. You think taking artifacts brings bad luck. *Tu es superstitieux, Jake, et tu ne peux pas me dire quoi faire.*"

She turned on her heel and moved away as Jake translated her words with difficulty: You are superstitious, Jake, and you can't tell me what to do.

She might as well have stabbed him with her diving knife. Jake was torn between believing he'd said the right thing, and wishing he'd kept his thoughts to himself and just admired the pretty bracelet on her slim arm. He felt humiliated by her words, and angry at himself. Slowly, a dull ache of realization began to form: that any hopes he'd been harboring about her being attracted to him were nothing but a figment of his imagination.

10   Channel Surprises

By noon, the three had finished most of the food in the cabin. They'd also patrolled the beaches on a regular basis. With each circuit around the island, Peter noticed, their steps toward the lookouts grew more frantic and their faces as they drew away from them grew longer. They'd agreed to swim across the channel this afternoon, but they each knew that the cold and the currents posed possible dangers. It had been one thing to swim across the channel yesterday knowing the *Adrienne* was a short distance away. But today, things were much different. No one was bringing up the topic most on their minds: where were the captain and Gavin? And why wasn't anyone searching for them?

Even if their dinghy had run out of gas after the first search, which had probably happened while they were waiting for high tide in the cave, they'd have returned to the sloop, refueled, and tried again. And by now, they'd surely have radioed the Coast Guard to launch a search. Yet there had been no boat or plane activity within sight of their island yesterday evening or this morning. Something was fishy about their situation.

But Peter prided himself on looking on the bright side of any situation—fishy or otherwise. He was, after all, trapped on a deserted island with a beautiful French girl. He'd be nuts not to try to take advantage of the circumstances. Unfortunately, Valerie had been a little too wily to let him corner her for a little kissing during beach patrol twosomes while Jake was elsewhere. She seemed to know just when he was about to make a move on her, and she'd sidestep him as adroitly as a seal sinking beneath the surface when kayakers headed its way. She was clearly playing hard to get. But never mind. Peter was patient, and he always won them over in the end. Didn't he?

"Peter and Jake, you eat octopus sometime?" Valerie was asking them. Peter watched the morning sunshine glint on her new bracelet. She'd been so excited about it, he'd decided not to let on that most people around here returned things like that to the band offices. But what did French girls know about band offices, and anyway, it looked pretty on her. Then again, anything looked pretty on her.

"Not me," Jake said.

"Octopus?" Peter asked distractedly, remembering the big octopus they'd seen on the ocean floor yesterday. "Yeah, grilled octopus is good. With wild rice and roasted peppers and …"

"Okay, this is what we must have for lunch," Valerie said, gathering up her hair and snapping a band around it. Okay, *that* comment had Peter's attention for sure. "Follow me," she said. He and Jake traipsed down the beach behind her to where small waves were slapping the shore. Peter followed closely, wondering what this exotic French girl was up to. He smirked at the sight of her wetsuit-bootie clad feet, boys' shorts, and pink nightie sneaking out from under the suspenders. She had to be the sexiest shipwreck victim he'd ever trailed along a beach, that was for sure.

He halted as she waded into the water up to her hips along a rocky wall and stooped to examine it just below the water level. The boys waded in behind her. Peter watched her eyes lock on a cavity about a foot wide. A tiny pile of rocks and shells sat along its outer edge, as if someone who lived there had just finished sweeping her house. With no warning, Valerie plunged her entire arm into the hole. Her eyebrows bunched up, her mouth pushed into a straining pout, then a smile broke and she pulled her arm out. A small octopus waved its legs—or were they arms?—

beneath her clenched fist. With a victorious smile, she pounded the octopus hard several times on the rock wall, the way a fisherman lowers a mallet on a fish's head to end its life as quickly and painlessly as possible. Then she marched back up to the cabin, the boys at her heels, plopped it into a bowl, and put a pot of water on to boil. She searched the cupboards until she found an old wine-bottle cork and dropped that into the pot, too.

"Tenderizes it," she told them.

"You're going to boil it?" Peter had to ask. He felt stupid the minute he'd said it. How else would one cook an octopus, especially when this cabin's residents hadn't thought to leave a barbecue grill and bottle of marinade around?

"But of course. Sorry I have no peppers to grill, but rice is here," she replied with a smile. "Perhaps we add nettles and berries."

"I'll make the rice and bring in some nettles and berries," Jake offered.

"Right then. I'll just go dig in the garden for carrots," Peter joked. He headed out of the cabin and veered for the outhouse. As he was sitting in the strangely oversized structure, he happened to look up and see what looked like the nose of a surfboard in its eaves. Funny place to hide a surfboard, he thought. Then again, if I had a cabin on an island likely to be visited by snoopy strangers, maybe I'd hide my board well, too. He returned to the kitchen and walked out with a kitchen chair, causing the cooks to raise their eyebrows. He slammed down the outhouse hole lid and perched the chair on top of it. He climbed up and scratched his head. Not one, but three old, yellowed boards were hidden there, complete with leashes. He hauled them down, one by one, and inspected them. One longboard and two shortboards. A few cracks and dings here and there. They were lightweight enough that he knew the foam inside wasn't water-logged. They seemed perfectly functional. He pulled them out into the sunlight and paused to look at the ocean. He, Jake, and Valerie all had their wetsuits. He knew just how to put his find to use.

Half an hour later, as they savored Valerie's surprisingly delicious nettle-berry-octopus dish with rice, Peter announced his plan. "I think we should put on our wetsuits and swim fins, and use the surfboards to cross the dolphin channel to the steep island," he stated. "Then we can hike around the point and shout to the *Adrienne*."

"A perfect plan!" Valerie cried, jumping up and shaking his hand. He'd have preferred a kiss, but she could always deliver that later, when Jake wasn't around.

"I agree," Jake said, smiling widely. "If they aren't coming here, we'll swim back to them. The boards will make that a lot easier. Especially the longboard. It has more flotation and waterline, so it'll paddle faster."

They waited until their lunch had settled, then toted their gear to the east side of the cabin's island. Peter noticed an afternoon wind rippling the previously glassy channel. They suited up and pushed in. Though they tried to stick close together, Valerie soon fell a little behind. Peter let Jake pass him as he waited for Valerie to close the gap, but he didn't want to get too far behind Jake, either. As they neared the western beach of the steep island, he looked back again.

How'd she get that far behind? She was hardly moving her arms. She'd climbed entirely onto her longboard and was crouched there on her knees, surveying the water around her, looking terrified. Hadn't Jake told her that sharks weren't a problem here? Maybe she'd mistaken a friendly seal for a sea lion?

"Valerie!" he shouted, but she didn't respond or lift her head, just kept staring into the deep water around her, frozen into inaction. She had barely reached mid-channel and had another ten minutes' paddling to go. Peter sighed and turned his board around to paddle back to her. That's when he saw the blur of black and white beneath the water, and saw a fin break the surface. That's no shark fin, he thought. And it's not a dolphin's fin either. It's much steeper and blacker. It has to be an orca, otherwise known as a killer whale.

Peter glanced back to see that Jake had reached shore. His friend was staring curiously at Peter and Valerie, trying to figure out what was taking them so long. Peter wasn't concerned because he knew that orcas have never been known to bother surfers. In the rare, privileged event that a killer whale pod passes a bay where people are surfing, the surfers always move out of their way until they pass. He'd heard only one unsubstantiated story of a surfer who'd felt threatened by an orca, and in the end, that orca had moved away without hurting him. The guy had probably been exaggerating.

Something else Peter knew: Orcas don't usually travel alone. They're generally in tight packs, a mother and her offspring. "Valerie," Peter called out. "It won't hurt you. Just paddle over to me." But as he said it, the fin passed between him and Valerie again. This was not normal orca behavior, as far as he knew, and he wasn't going to push his luck paddling closer to the eight-ton creature, beautiful and harmless as it might be.

Valerie hadn't moved, and her board was beginning to drift backward. "Valerie," Peter shouted in irritation, "it's an orca. It's not interested in you."

As if in response, the orca burst out of the water and breached between Peter and Valerie. Its eyes were clearly on Valerie, its teeth were showing, and if Peter had ever seen malevolence in a creature, he was seeing it now. Valerie wasn't imagining anything. And that surfer boy probably hadn't been exaggerating either. No one would ever believe them, but Peter knew with helpless horror that this orca was all business, and for no good reason, its business was separating the boys from Valerie.

Peter heard Valerie begin screaming as he instinctively backed away. Jake, he could see, was standing on shore with his mouth open. Valerie turned and began paddling back to the cabin island. Peter watched her all the way and saw the fin only once more, this time carrying on north up the channel. As he watched Valerie scramble up the shore, he hesitated. Well, might as well join Jake and do what we came here for, he reasoned. Get to the other side of this island and get the attention of the *Adrienne*. Then they could come round with the dinghy and pick up Valerie.

"I wouldn't believe it if I hadn't seen it," Peter said as he reached Jake.

"Never heard of anything like it," Jake agreed. "Maybe Valerie got between a mother and its baby or something?"

"No sign of that," Peter said.

"Well, she's safe now, and she knows we'll be back for her as soon as we can. Let's go see what's up with our lazy rescuers."

The island was so steep they couldn't cross over its

top. They had to make their way through jumbles of shore rocks to the south end. As they rounded the point, the boys stopped and stared, aghast.

"It's gone," they spoke together. "Totally. Gone."

They looked east across the three-mile watery expanse to the coast, a distance so great that its trees were barely visible. The seas were much rougher here. No sign of anything on shore, Peter judged, though they'd have needed binoculars to see much anyway.

"They wouldn't have left us," Jake spoke adamantly.

"But they did," Peter said incredulously. "They lifted anchor and went, just like that. Gave up on us with hardly a look. Maybe didn't even contact the Coast Guard. Doesn't seem possible."

Jake shook his head and sank to the ground. Neither spoke for a while.

"Jake," Peter finally said, "there's regular boat traffic along this channel, and native communities along the mainland's coast. We have to paddle our surfboards into this channel and hope for a boat to see us, or continue on to the mainland."

"By mainland you mean the west coast of Vancouver Island?"

"Of course."

"Okay, but not right now," Jake said, looking alarmed. "We have to go back and get Valerie. And this channel won't be like the small one we just crossed.

It's a long way to the mainland."

True, Peter thought. And it's exposed, with deadly rip currents all over the place. He'd heard the captain and first mate discussing that. But rip currents don't steal sixty-three-foot sloops. He shook his head, still stunned that the men weren't here.

"Let's not make Valerie anymore scared than she is," Peter said. "Time to get back."

This time they made the crossing in less than ten minutes, with only one or two worried looks into the water beneath them. There was no sign of a lone mad orca, nor playful dolphins, nor anything else for that matter. Which suited Peter just fine.

11   Eight Arms

"**I** never cross that channel again," Valerie declared, hands on her hips and her face as emotional as Jake had ever seen it. The three were standing in the cabin's kitchen. "Especially not with Peter. He leaves me in middle and goes on!" She turned an enraged expression on Peter, who flinched a little, glanced at Jake with a raised eyebrow, and strolled out the cabin door.

"Valerie," Jake said gently, reaching for her hands, which she allowed him to take in his, "it was a freak thing. Peter saw the orca swimming off after you had turned around. It didn't hurt you, and it's not still hanging around. That was just a weird, freaky show of behavior. I guess we can't explain everything in nature." He was rubbing her arm to reassure her, when his hand touched the copper bracelet. Both their eyes went down to it. There was an awkward pause.

It would be disrespectful to touch that, maybe even bad luck. It's not yours to take, he had told her.

She lifted her eyes to his with a pleading look. "You will paddle very close to me if I cross channel again, Jake? You will look out for me?"

Jake's heart leapt as her eyes stayed on his. "Of course I will," he promised.

She withdrew one of her hands from his, and in one swift move, removed the copper bracelet. Still watching him, she said, "Sorry I spoke not so nicely earlier, Jake. Maybe you were right about bracelet." Her face softened and she leaned closer to him. "You wear it until we are back to Tofino, Jake."

Before he could say anything, she clamped it onto his arm, gave him a peck on the cheek, and stepped away, eyes smiling now. "How far again, between the island where *Adrienne* was and mainland?"

"About three miles. Five kilometers. A one-hour swim if all goes right." He hoped she didn't catch the note of worry in his voice about all going right. He'd normally never consider crossing such an exposed stretch of water, even in a kayak.

"Then we should leave it till tomorrow morning. Is too late this afternoon, and maybe will be less windy in morning," she said.

Jake's face was warm, and the place where she'd planted the kiss was burning pleasantly red hot. He stepped forward to take Valerie in his arms, but she whirled around at just the wrong second and dashed out the door. "I find some clams," she announced. "Maybe you hunt another *poulpe pour souper*, I mean octopus, for dinner."

Fifteen minutes later, Jake floated along the beach, his heart two sizes larger than normal. She'd shouted angrily at Peter and kissed him, Jake Evans. A peck on the cheek, really, but that was a kiss. What more could he ask?

Anyone in Peter's position would have backed away from a threatening animal, but the bizarre event had worked in Jake's favor. Orcas probably didn't visit southwestern France on a regular basis, and Valerie was understandably upset by its strange behavior. Anyway, she was all his now. That's all that mattered. She'd declared her love with the bracelet, even if wearing it made Jake feel a little uneasy. Was it bad luck? Nah. And Peter would get over his passing interest in Valerie. Peter had his pick of girls anywhere, anytime, and Valerie was too special for a ladies' man like Peter.

It was low tide, perfect for octopus hunting. Jake ran his eyes along the flat portion of the reef where Valerie had caught her octopus and waded in up to his chest. He searched hard for a hole with a pile of debris pushed to one side, like the one that his clever Valerie had been so quick to detect. She'd challenged him to bring home an octopus, and he was going to spear one for her. Or at least, lift it up by its wriggling legs and deliver it to her kitchen. The delicious taste of this afternoon's octopus was still on his tongue, and the afternoon's journey across the channel and back had worked up his appetite.

The channel. Jake tried hard to close his mind to the question of why the men had left them. What could the three stranded divers do about it now? They had to fend for themselves. Peter was right. They'd flag down a boat in the big channel, or if worst came to worst, they'd arm-paddle all the way to the mainland and find one of the small communities along the coast. Someone would take them in, phone Nancy, and solve the mystery of the *Adrienne*. She'd charter a water taxi and come get them the minute she heard from them. It would all turn out okay.

Aha! He spied a cavity in the reef, and the telltale sweepings of what could only be a major neat-freak octopus. For a second, he even saw the wave of a red tentacle. It reminded him of a cat's tail thumping from behind a sofa, as the cat lay convinced it was hidden from view.

Heart beating, he thrust his arm in, felt the globular head. "Ow!" he yowled as the octopus's beak nipped him, but he wouldn't let go. No way. Mighty hunters ignore small wounds inflicted while catching supper for their family. It was just part of the job. He moved his hand around the lumpy head, which felt very large indeed, and began to tug.

That's when the tentacles flew up his arm and wrapped themselves around it. Jake couldn't believe the power of the grip. For a second, he considered letting the creature be, but then he remembered that Valerie's pot was waiting for his catch. She'd merely plucked her little guy out and slammed it against the rocks.

He gave a terrific yank to pull his arm out, octopus and all, but this giant was having none of it. It wouldn't budge, and Jake, strong as he was, couldn't move it an inch. Jake was feeling a little cold. He didn't have his wetsuit on, and the tide was creeping up his chest, an occasional wave reaching up to slap his chin.

"Look, buddy, it's you or me," Jake tried to joke. "And I can't breathe under water, so it's going to have to be you—now."

He strained and pulled with everything he had, and was shocked to find that he really couldn't pull the thing out. His arm was totally stuck in there as long as that octopus decided to hang on. It must be many times the size of Valerie's octopus, he realized slowly, fearfully. They can grow to near man-sized, he remembered. Wasn't there a movie about a giant octopus that clamped itself around an entire submarine? But that was science fiction. This was real.

Jake's teeth were starting to chatter, and he was blowing bubbles through some wave tosses now. The tide was coming in quickly, and it would be only minutes before he'd be under. He looked up and down the beach, but there was no sign of Valerie or Peter.

"Valerie! Peter!" he yelled while inserting his other hand into the cavity as far as he could, and attempting to extract the tentacles from his arm. He could loosen the end of one, but the minute he started working on another, the first would tighten again. He had only one free arm. His challenger had eight, each nearly as long as Jake's, and evidently much stronger.

"Okay, you win," Jake told it in a slightly squeaky voice as a new surge of water brought the ocean's surface to chin level. "Let go and you're free."

The octopus remained locked on.

A wave pushed over Jake's head. He held his breath, put both his feet against the reef, and used his entire body as leverage to pull his captive arm out. The octopus only seemed to latch tighter. Spluttering and turning his face to the sky, he managed to get his mouth above water to breathe. He tried yelling for his companions again but knew now they weren't going to save him. He recalled the story of a hiker forced to cut off his own arm when it became trapped under a fallen rock. He had nothing on him to do damage to the octopus or himself.

The next set of cold, salty waves again forced him to hold his breath under water, and for a time he thought this was going to be it.

Relax. He didn't know where the message came from—the ocean, his mind, or maybe even the octopus. But it seemed like a new strategy, so he closed his eyes and forced himself to relax. He had to work hard at a visual image of relaxing the arm tightly wrapped in tentacles. But as he pushed the tension out of his arm, he felt the tentacles unlatch, one by one, from upper to lower arm. He managed to pull his arm out part of the way. But a new surge of tide forced him to hold his breath and he sank down to the level of the little cavity. Groping about, he felt the lower tentacles still firmly suctioned onto the copper bracelet. Chest pounding with lack of breath, he reached forward, popped the bracelet off, and felt himself float up to the surface. The octopus had won its life and the bracelet. But Jake was alive, eyes stinging from the saltwater.

Being free wasn't the same as being safe, he suddenly realized. His feet could no longer touch the bottom, and he was floundering in the surf with no wetsuit or board. He was truly feeling the chill. He was also determined not to be washed out to sea.

With the next set of waves, he bodysurfed through the pounding shorebreak, leapt to his feet, and ran for his life, not stopping for a second until he was at the cabin's door.

12   Unrest

Peter was scouring the kitchen cupboards for any food they may have missed on their first pass. Under the empty sugar bowl inside the kitchen cupboard was something almost as good.

"A key!" he exclaimed to Valerie as she stirred her pot of clams on the hotplate. "I'm going to see what it fits." He remembered seeing a lock on a cupboard somewhere outside. They hadn't gotten around to deciding if it was worth breaking into. "Mmmm, those clams smell good," he added, poking his chin over her shoulder and pretending to study the pot.

She giggled and raised her wooden spoon threateningly. "*Vas t'en.* Go away, Peter Montpetit, until my dinner is ready. It still needs an octopus, which is coming soon, I think."

"An octopus with eight arms," Peter said, wrapping his arms around her and waving them about like tentacles.

"I chop off octopus arms," she said sternly, tapping her wooden spoon on his wrists none too gently.

"Leave her alone!" Jake's voice sounded from the doorway.

Peter dropped his arms to his sides, whirled around, and stared at Jake. For a second, he thought Jake might be angry that he and Valerie had been messing around. Then it dawned on him that Jake was shivering, wet from head to toe, and white-faced.

"You look half-drowned! Did you fall in the water?" Peter asked.

"Jake, what has happened?" Valerie said, grabbing a towel from a nearby hook and rushing over to hand it to him.

Jake took the towel, directed a scowl at Peter, and marched into the bedroom. He emerged minutes later in dry clothing. He sat down and told them the most outrageous octopus story Peter had ever heard. Peter believed him, alright, especially when Valerie said she'd heard of a French snorkeler who'd had a similar experience. "You must relax arm or they won't let go," she murmured, face filled with concern for Jake.

"That's what finally worked, but even then, it still had hold of the bracelet, so I had to remove it to get free."

There was a long pause. Peter was thinking, what bracelet? Jake didn't wear a bracelet.

"So you had to remove it, but you still have it, yes?"

Valerie asked, her dark eyes intent on his face.

Valerie's bracelet? Peter wondered. But why would Jake have had that on? Surely Valerie would never let that thing out of her sight.

"No, I don't still have it," Jake said with a touch of exasperation. "It's gone. In the octopus's hole."

Peter watched Valerie's eyes open wide. When she banged her wooden spoon down on the pot of boiling clams, he jumped.

"So you lose my bracelet and bring us no octopus?" she accused Jake with what Peter thought was shocking meanness. Hadn't Jake just explained that he'd almost drowned? What was with Valerie?

Jake's mouth slid a little open, but nothing came out. He tried again. "Valerie, if you had a choice between drowning or shedding a …"

"You lose my bracelet!" Valerie roared. She looked to Peter for support, but he just stared at her. Eyes flashing, she banged her spoon again, then plunged it into the pot and ran out of the cabin.

Jake and Peter looked at each other. Peter was wordless, plus he felt uncomfortable under what seemed an increasingly hostile gaze from his best buddy. Was he missing something here? Struggling to make sense of it, he formed a hurried theory that tumbled from his lips.

"Jake, remember how you told Valerie she had no

right to take that bracelet, and that it might bring her bad luck?"

Jake continued to glare at him. "So I say stupid things sometimes. What's that got to do with anything?"

"Maybe she gave it to you because she thought that orca incident was her bad luck for wearing it. And now she thinks that the octopus was bad luck for you, and she's kind of scared."

"She didn't look scared to me," Jake said, voice raised.

"No, she looked mad. But girls do that. When they're scared, they act mad."

Jake stared at Peter, then sneered. As the pot on the stove began boiling over, he stood up and lowered the heat, and began stirring with the spoon.

"Or maybe she's mad that you're harassing her, Mr. Thinks-He's-Hot. Why don't you take a hint and disappear? From her, from me, from us. Get it?"

Peter blinked. Where had that come from? He was definitely missing something here. Better to retreat and think it over. He looked down and saw the key he'd found under the sugar bowl still in his hand. He shrugged and gave Jake what he hoped was a suitably wounded look. Then he stepped outside and wandered around the building until he found a locked cupboard.

Excellent! The key fit the lock. He swung open the

rickety door. A couple of musty tarps. Some rusty tools, including an ax. A sturdy gardening shovel. A faded plastic pail. And what looked like a packed-away tent. He yanked the tent out, shook it out of its bag, and started snapping the poles together. Not because anyone needed a tent, but because he didn't know what else to do. Then again, if everyone was going to be mad at each other for no reason—at least, no reason he could fathom—maybe a tent might serve as a handy extra room. It was one of those domed tents, he decided as he erected it. But the fabric was pretty past it: ripped and as moldy as month-old bread. He refolded the fabric and returned it to the cupboard, then gazed at the assembled poles, scratching his head.

He squatted down and stared at the tent's skeleton some more, just because he was a little afraid to go back into the kitchen, clam supper or not. And slowly, that dome gave him an idea. He picked it up and walked down to the beach with it. Then he returned for the shovel and tarps. Back at the beach, he dug a hole a foot deep and two feet across, set the dome over it, and hung the tarps over the dome to make a little tent. Next he gathered some wood and three large rocks.

"What are you making, new *toilette*?" Valerie asked as she wandered by. He noticed she wasn't wet, and she hadn't retrieved her bracelet. He'd half expected her to go give that octopus a piece of her mind until it anted up. But maybe she'd cooled off and gotten some sense into that *très jolie* head of hers.

"I'm making a sauna," Peter said proudly.

"A sauna?"

"Yup. I'm going to build a fire, heat some rocks until they're red hot, then move them by shovel into that hole under the dome. Then we'll spill water over the rocks to make them steam, and sit in the tent around the rocks till we can't take the heat any more."

She smiled. "Then we take flying leap into ocean to cool off and return for more?"

"You got it! And maybe build up the fire, too, for catching the attention of a plane or boat."

"This sounds fun. But maybe we eat clams before we make sauna."

"Excellent idea. And Valerie," he said, putting on a soft, maybe even suave voice.

She looked at him warily.

"How about some surfing tonight? The waves are getting bigger. It's starting to look kinda fun out there."

She turned and took in the surf, then nodded enthusiastically. "*Oui*, Peter. Let's go for surf tonight."

Jake still looked a little grumpy when Peter and Valerie stepped in the door together, but he did spoon the clams into some bowls and they sat down to eat together.

"Peter and I are going for surf after supper. Will you also come?" Valerie asked Jake.

Jake looked from one to the other, eyes a little slanted. It crossed Peter's mind that Valerie still kind of owed Jake an apology about the bracelet outburst, but he sure wasn't going to interfere on that score. Still, Valerie's lack of apology might be why Jake shook his head no.

"I'm tired," he said. He sure looked tired to Peter. Who wouldn't be tired after a near drowning and an epic octopus battle?

Valerie put on a little pout for show and said, "You are sure?"

"Very sure," he said, eyes on the table, mouth drawn tight. Peter always tried to stay out of Jake's way when he got in one of his "down" moods. Jake also seemed to be avoiding Peter's eyes.

"Okay, but we'll come get you when the sauna is ready," Peter promised in as cheerful a voice as he could muster. He loved the look of surprise that flashed across Jake's face. "I've built a homemade sauna down on the beach with an old dome tent frame and some tarps. Just what we need tonight, before we paddle out to get rescued in the morning. A nice, relaxing sauna."

That coaxed a smile out of Jake, which pleased Peter. He and Peter had built saunas on camping trips before. They were always good for fun, laughter, and relaxation. So, thought Peter, my sauna will make us a happy threesome again.

An hour later, he and Valerie changed into their wetsuits and toted the old shortboards down to the beach. The evening breeze raised goose pimples on Peter's back before he zipped up. What he wanted most was to impress Valerie, but she was pretty hot on a board, so he'd have to find some tricks she didn't know. Hey! Maybe he could teach her some new stuff.

The low sun cast a rosy glow on the head-high waves. They'd grown a few feet since before supper. It was building fast, which could mean some pretty wild stuff was coming their way. Or maybe it would settle down overnight. Impossible to know with no access to a surf or weather report. Not that local weather has a lot to do with surf. Peter knew that storms hundreds or thousands of miles out to sea can stir up angry forces that spend days charging toward a faraway shore.

Peter and Valerie walked through the white foam washing around their legs and laughed heartily as they jumped over incoming waves. Soon it was time to lie on the boards, paddle, and duck-dive when something big reared overhead. Finally, they made it to the outside. After catching and riding a few fun ones, Peter made sure Valerie was looking his way before trying a frontside air.

"*Bon,*" she complimented him, making Peter's chest expand.

"Want to try it?" he asked coaxingly.

"*Oui,* okay."

"Just try to pump for as much speed as you can get, and instead of kicking out of the wave, try to use it as a launch ramp when it closes out."

When the next wave came in, she took off, streaked down the line, and managed to get her board off the top and into the air.

"*Très bien!* Very good!" he delivered his two best French words. "But next time, try staying higher on the wave. It's all about the speed."

She did, rose even higher the next time, and managed to stick the landing and ride out the wave.

"Okay, do you know how to stall for the barrel?"

"Peter, I don't know these English words." She laughed lightly.

"Oh, it's when you ride down the line, but instead of racing out in front, you slow yourself down and sneak under the lip as it starts to throw. Try it on one of these hollow ones, then do this," he said as he showed her how to drag an arm in the wave's face to get into the tube. "And when the wave starts to arc over you, keep your eyes open so you can see where to escape." Peter was guessing that as experienced a recreational surfer as Valerie was, she might not be familiar with a more extreme move like that.

She looked behind her, presumably waiting for a wave that looked like it would jack up and barrel onto the shore. Then, looking just a little nervous, she paddled hard and took off. The wave swooped her up and seemed to swallow her as she stalled, pulled in, and then shot out onto the shoulder as the wave exploded.

"Awesome, awesome, awesome!" Peter cheered her on, stoked about her wave and pleased he'd managed to come up with something she didn't already know.

"Awesome is better than *très bien?*" she joked.

"Awesome is way better than *très bien!*"

He found time to teach her some more tricks, then graciously accepted her coaching on a move he hadn't seen before: switching stance going backside.

After he pulled it off, all he could think was, We're happening. We're made for each other. But hardly had the thought entered his mind than an unsettled feeling followed it. Jake. That was it. Jake was imagining that Valerie was his. If so, Jake was dreaming. But Jake was his best friend. Maybe it wasn't such a good idea to win Valerie for himself, even if he was sure that was just what she wanted.

"It is nearly dark," Valerie finally pointed out.

She was right. Time to exit the tossing waves and get that sauna fired up.

13   The Sauna

Jake loved saunas. They not only cleansed a person's skin; they had a way of coaxing negative feelings right out of one's pores and washing them away. He didn't want to dwell on the little scene with Valerie. Clearly, she hadn't understood how dangerous the situation had been. Or, like Peter had said, maybe she'd been so frightened of how close Jake had come to drowning, that things had come out all wrong; she'd said things she was now surely regretting.

As for Peter and Valerie, Jake knew that Peter was deluding himself that Valerie liked him. Let him try to act like Mr. You-Can't-Resist-Me. He'd get bored with it pretty soon. He was used to easy catches. Anyway, now that Peter knew Valerie had given Jake the bracelet, surely he understood where things stood and would back away. Maybe he'd even be happy for Jake. Peter knew very well that Jake had never had a girlfriend before. Once he got used to the idea, he'd slap Jake on the shoulder and wish him hearty congratulations. Yup, that would be Peter's way.

"More water," Peter ordered.

"I'll get it!" Jake volunteered. He jumped out, ducked under the door flap of their steamy little dome, and fetched a pail of seawater. When he returned, Peter shone his diving flashlight on the pile of hot rocks to make sure Jake wouldn't stumble against them while slowly emptying his pail. The hissing brought with it a wonderful billow of fresh steam. Jake stuck his face in it, savoring the heat. "Better than a five-star hotel," he declared.

"Not quite," Valerie responded. She, like the boys, was wearing only the one-piece swimsuit she'd had on under her wetsuit when they'd left the *Adrienne*. Jake thought she looked great in it.

"So what did you learn from Coach Peter today?" Jake asked her, trying not to stare and wondering if maybe he should have found the energy to join them.

"Oh, Peter tells me how to 'stall for the barrel.' Barrel is when a hollow wave breaks right over a surfer, yes? And to 'stall for it' is to slow yourself down to keep yourself inside it, yes? I drag a hand behind me or push my arm into the wave like brake."

Jake raised an eyebrow. "He did tell you, I hope, that if you go for something like that, you can get really worked."

"What means 'really worked'?"

"Have a heavy, painful wipeout. Only heavy, steep waves barrel. So barreling waves are the most dangerous, and stalling is one of the hardest moves, even if pulling it off is the ultimate ride."

"Oh," Valerie said, pulling her knees closer to her chest and giving Peter a sideways glance. "No, he did not explain me this."

"But she's a natural," Peter said proudly—and, Jake thought, a little defensively.

They went silent for a moment, taking in the pounding of the surf outside their shelter.

"It's getting big," Peter spoke up.

And it was, Jake noticed, peeking out the sauna door. The surf was really starting to roar. Salt spray from the breaking waves was starting to drift through the air. "Could be killer stuff tomorrow," Jake suggested.

"Maybe too big to surf?" Valerie asked in a tight voice.

"We're not surfing," Peter observed. "We're belly-riding to the open channel and flagging down a boat. I bet we'll hardly be out there long enough to get cold."

Jake thought that sounded dangerously optimistic, but he wanted off this island, too. "Tomorrow's Monday," he observed soberly. "We're supposed to be back to guide the clients. Nancy is expecting us tomorrow."

Peter sighed. "We are guiding one of the clients, and we will be back tomorrow. She didn't say what time," he added mischievously.

"I still don't get it," Jake said. "No *Adrienne*, no dinghy, no Coast Guard helicopters or search boats. It's like the *Adrienne* sank without a trace the minute we got around the corner of the first island, taking everyone with it." He shook his head, not believing it was possible, nor being willing to state the only other theory: that the captain and Gavin had left them stranded on purpose. They'd never do that. Why would they?

"We've been over and over it," Peter mumbled, drawing up his knees, resting his elbows on them, and lowering his head to his arms. "Nothing makes sense. All we can count on is that no one ever put out a call on us. There's no one missing us." He shot a glance out the sauna tent to the sky as if to make certain.

"This is why we are surfing to mainland in the morning. We will be okay," Valerie tried to cheer them up.

They gazed at the rocks in silence.

"How big do waves get around here?" Valerie asked.

"I heard some dude in Tofino say thirty feet during storms," Jake replied. "And then there was the tsunami here in 1964. Not as big as the Southeast Asian tsunami in 2004, but major."

"I wonder what the biggest wave ever surfed is?" Peter mused.

"Forty feet—that's four stories," Jake replied. "That was during The Swell of 1969 at Kaena Point in Hawaii, by some world-famous surfer named Greg 'Da Bull' Noll, I think."

"Forty feet? That's humungous. That's ugly. That's insane," said Peter.

"What means 'humungous'?" Valerie shivered and wrapped her arms around her shoulders. "Never mind; I can guess. Actually some people have surf seventy-foot waves."

"You're right, but that was surfers being slingshot in," said Peter, "using tow lines behind jet skis."

"Humungous, ugly, and insane," Valerie declared, sending the boys into guffaws of laughter.

"How to surf a four-story wave?" Valerie asked.

Jake wasn't going to answer that, but it didn't surprise him when Peter spoke up.

"Not that I've ever surfed one, or would ever surf one, but if I had to, I'd try to get barreled," Peter mused. "I've watched some of the crazy guys in Hawaii find the tube on fifty-footers at Jaws. Jaws is the name of one of Hawaii's best surf spots. There's nothing better in surfing. That's as good as it gets."

"Our rocks are getting cold," Jake said as he tipped another helping of water on their setup but it elicited only a weak puff of steam.

"Yeah, it's not a five-star sauna or we'd have servants out there heating up some more rocks for us," Peter admitted.

"Anyway, we need good rest tonight," Valerie suggested. "Tomorrow could be very interesting, no?"

"I'm voting for boring," Jake kidded her, offering his hand to help her up. She smiled and rose by herself, and the three filed out. They stood in front of their homemade sauna.

"We need to put the poles and tarps back where we found 'em," Peter said. "Let's forget about building up the fire. I've given up on rescuers, and we all need a good night's sleep."

Jake took the flashlight from Peter and flicked it off. They watched the wind-whipped waves by moonlight for a long time.

"Wind is coming from the south," Valerie observed.

"See the halo around the moon," Jake said, motioning to a hazy circle around their light source. "Doesn't that mean a change of weather coming?"

"Maybe," Peter said, shrugging his shoulders.

Jake's eyes returned to the water, where they became transfixed. Waves are like flames dancing in a fire, he thought. They can put you in a trance. They create ever-changing colors and patterns. But unlike fires, they never die. They just keep coming and coming and coming. He flicked the flashlight back on and started back to the cabin, accompanied by a vigorous chorus of frogs and crickets.

"Valerie, would you like to know the temperature right now?" Jake asked, excited to remember something from a science class that he knew would impress her.

"*Oui*, Jake, but how do you know?" she responded.

"The crickets will tell us. Count their chirps for exactly fourteen seconds. Peter, can you use your watch to signal us when fourteen seconds is up? Ready, go."

The three counted cricket chirps until Peter's raised arm fell.

"Twenty," Valerie reported, face turned to Jake expectantly.

"Now add forty, and that's the air temperature in Fahrenheit," he declared in his most authoritative voice. "Sixty. That's fifteen Celsius."

"A good August night temperature, I think," Valerie said, face lit by the moonlight.

When they reached the cabin, Jake didn't feel tired at all. He spied a dusty corner with a handful of books and began fingering through them for something interesting.

"Finding us some bedtime reading?" Peter asked. "I'm not tired either."

"No bedtime reading here unless you like *The Farmers' Almanac*, *A Guide to Insects*, or *West Coast Legends*.

"*West Coast Legends*," Valerie voted.

Jake hopped onto his bed and sat cross-legged with

the flashlight trained on the yellowed pages. He flipped through the book, then stopped. "Here's a good section. 'Though coastal aboriginal people of British Columbia hunted some species of whales, they always revered and respected the spirit and majesty of the killer whale, also known as orca. They believed that the souls of departed noble chiefs and great hunters resided in them.'"

"It wasn't a very noble chief who came after Valerie today," Peter commented dryly, crossing his legs on his mattress and resting his back against the wall behind him.

"Peter, don't interrupt," Valerie chastised him.

"'But some mythic killer whales were malicious,'" Jake continued reading. "'They were changed into reefs, and their dorsal fins, now hardened to rock, continue to threaten sea-faring folk.'" The dorsal fin-shaped island nearby flashed into Jake's mind. Hadn't the dolphins and the bad-tempered killer whale passed right by it? Maybe the noble chief-turned-orca knew Valerie had taken his bracelet. Okay, that was a silly thought. He glanced at her furrowed brow and wondered if he should switch to *The Farmers' Almanac*.

"More," she urged quietly.

"'The sea monster named Sisiutl roamed the land and sea of the Kwakiutl peoples …'"

"Hey, this is getting better," Peter said, sprawling full length on his bed and tucking his hands under his chin. "A sea monster local to this area."

"Actually," Jake corrected him, "to the area a hundred miles north of us. Anyway," he continued reading, "'a dramatic supernatural creature, the double-headed sea serpent is one of the high-ranking crests of the Kwagiulth culture. Touching or even looking at the serpent can cause death.'"

"Like, instant death?" Peter asked, bouncing back to a sitting position.

"By turning to stone, if you'd let me read," Jake said impatiently. "'A warrior would often wear a head band or belt in the image of a Sisiutl to provide protection from harm. Flakes of shiny mica found on beaches were thought to be the discarded scales from the serpent's body. Sisiutl guarded the entrances to the homes of the supernatural.'"

"All of British Columbia is supernatural," Peter panned, quoting a tourism advertisement. No one laughed.

"What is mica?" Valerie asked, eyes wide.

"Shiny stuff in rocks. It looks like glitter," Jake explained. He slammed the book shut and coughed at the dust that was raised. He didn't like Peter's high-spiritedness or Valerie's look of concern. "Lights out, kids. Flashlight batteries are going, anyway."

No one argued. As the three castaways crawled under their covers, the wind whistled and the surf pounded, lulling them to sleep quickly. Jake dreamed of surfing right in front of a two-headed serpent whose bad breath dripped mica on him. He and Peter knew not to turn around and look at it, but he couldn't stop his Valerie from spinning around once to peek. As she turned to stone, the waves reared higher and higher, pounding against her. He awoke, sweating. *Just a dream.* He threw his covers off and crept to the cabin's window. The wind was strong, but not battering. The moonlit surf pounded the shore with the same steady beat they'd heard from inside the sauna.

The dream had left him with a powerful feeling of dread. He never should have let Valerie wear that bracelet or give it to him to wear.

14   Storm Waves

When Jake awoke at daybreak, he listened carefully. The wind was blowing, but no harder than the night before. He climbed out of bed and looked out the window to their exposed western beachfront. Head-high waves were rising and crashing, but the surf wasn't outrageous. In fact, it looked rather inviting. Not that they'd be surfing there. They'd be paddling out from the more sheltered eastern side of the island. He raised his eyes to the sky. It was blue with a striking dark-red tinge. The kind a watercolorist might love to set up an easel to paint.

"How looks it?" Valerie spoke sleepily from under her covers.

"*Super,*" Jake replied. "*Un café, mademoiselle?*"

"Make that three coffees, *garçon,*" Peter spoke up from his mattress. "We'll need the warmth in our guts out there no matter what it's doing."

"If you think it's one hour to swim across, then safest time to try this is one hour before slack tide," Valerie noted. "That would be middle of this morning."

"Good calculating," Jake said.

By the agreed-upon time, the trio had consumed a large bowl full of huckleberries Valerie had gathered, and two cups of coffee each. They'd cleaned the cabin vigorously, folded their borrowed quilts and clothes back into drawers, restocked the equipment cupboard with equipment exactly as they'd found it, and left a thank you note explaining about the food and surfboards. Jake penned that.

"When we get rescued," Jake said as he zipped up his wetsuit, "we'll get someone to swing by here to return the surfboards and replace the food, and retrieve the diving equipment at low tide."

"You are *très* thoughtful, Jake," Valerie observed.

Jake felt his face go warm as he smiled at her.

"You take the longboard again, Valerie," Peter suggested. "It'll keep you higher above water and be easier to paddle, especially if we get into big waves."

"We will have big waves?" Valerie asked, concerned.

"Hopefully not," Jake reassured her. "And I think it's important we all try to stay near one another."

"*Oui*," Valerie agreed, nodding her head soberly.

They carried their boards and swim fins to the northeastern tip of the island, then stuffed their swim fins inside their wetsuits and waded in. Jake had insisted they bring fins in case they ended up losing their boards and having to swim. The wind had died almost completely. Jake took this as a good sign. A large flock of seagulls crowded on the shore rocks as if to see the group off. They watched the boys with beady eyes and cocked beaks, protesting the invasion with a squawk or two, but not taking flight as Jake expected. He vaguely remembered Nancy saying that large seagull clusters meant something, but he couldn't remember what.

Jake stuck close to Valerie, knowing she would be nervous here, where they'd last seen the orca. The water between the cabin's island and the fin-shaped island was calm. As the three lay on their boards and put their arms into action, Jake knew it would be rougher going when they rounded the second island's northern point. Ten minutes later, all three paused to look down the eastern side of the fin-shaped island, as if hoping the *Adrienne* would have reappeared there since they'd last checked. No such luck. Nor was there any boat traffic between them and the mainland. Just an expanse of blue-gray swells, lifting and falling.

Far across, the trees looked the size of peanuts, but at least Jake could see them.

"You really think only one hour to mainland?" Valerie asked, pointing her board due east.

"One or two," Jake said, trying to put certainty into his tone as they entered the water.

"Why is the ocean blue one day, green the next, and then gray?" Peter spoke up as their arms churned the water.

"It takes its color from the sky," Jake said. He glanced overhead and saw that, indeed, the sky had changed from blue and red to blue and gray. *Red*, he thought. What was the line Valerie had taught them? "Red sky at night, sailor's delight. Red sky at morning, sailor's warning." He studied the sky. The red was gone, but the warning had been issued and he'd missed it at the time. He twisted his head back toward the second island they were leaving behind. A second flock of seagulls sat there, eyeing them solemnly. None were taking to the air. There was no reason to turn back, he decided.

The swells were kind of fun. At least, they would have been if Jake hadn't felt so exposed on all sides. They carried the surfers up, and they carried them down. *All we have to do is keep propelling ourselves forward,* Jake thought, *while this gentle roller coaster plays with us.* He reveled in working his muscles. He was strong and fit, and hadn't had any decent exercise since they'd shed their diving gear—unless one counted the octopus-wrestling match. He decided to look on the paddling as a workout. He dug in hard with a grin. He and Peter didn't need to hold back much for Valerie, because her board rode higher and easier. Anyway, who was in a hurry? They'd get there when they got there. It was just a matter of moving steadily forward.

Within minutes, however, the gentle roller coaster transformed into big, rolling swells, some more than twenty feet high. Though the gray, watery humps were not themselves a problem—the three could muscle their boards up and down them—the rising wind worried him. Soon, the top few feet of some swells became messy, jagged chop, seriously slowing their progress. Jake shook his head after breaking through one, and took a look around him. The sea was writhing as if infested with giant serpents just below the surface. He shot a look at Peter, whose expression returned the show of concern.

"We're not halfway yet," Jake noted, testing Peter's opinion on whether they should turn back.

"And we haven't seen a single boat since we started," Peter complained.

As Jake's board skidded down the backside of one wave and climbed sluggishly up the slope of the next, he noted that most of the swells ahead were now acquiring white tops. That was not a good thing. As the first drops of rain spattered his face, he realized the wind had accelerated to a blustering force.

"Jake, I think we are in storm *terrible*," Valerie called to him, her voice revealing a tremor.

"Jake, I think we should turn back," Peter said the next time the darkening ocean pitched them close to one another. "This is really heavy—really, really nasty."

Jake didn't like to admit defeat, but both the ocean and sky had turned menacing on them, faster than he had ever imagined possible. He was about to agree when Valerie's voice reached them.

"A boat!"

They all turned to see a faraway seine boat struggling north along the mainland's shoreline, as if looking for an inlet in which to harbor from the coming squall. It was a great distance away, but it was what they'd been waiting for. Jake raised his hand above his eyes, because the rain was now pelting so hard he could hardly see any distance, let alone stay focused on the shore. In between the surfboards and the fishing boat, the wind was now tearing the white crests off waves and flinging them about wildly. The three surfers stroked with everything they had, as if effort alone would make the tossing boat's operators spot them. But the vessel, whose windows were no doubt being pelted by horizontal rain, showed no sign of veering their way. Soon it was out of sight. The shore behind it seemed an unending stretch of ugly black, broken rock.

Peter and Jake looked at each other.

"We're pretty much at the halfway point now," Jake pronounced.

"We've been paddling for an hour," Peter reported.

"What must we do?" Valerie asked, arms hugging her board as if frightened of losing it in the giant swells now tossing them about.

"Let's try to make the mainland," Peter ruled. "There must be some bay we can surf into safely."

Getting through the shore break is going to be freaky, Jake worried, but neither he nor Valerie disagreed with Peter.

"Everyone warm enough?" Jake asked, trying to hide the beginnings of his own shivering.

"I am okay," Valerie volunteered. Of course, riding higher on her board, she should be, Jake thought. Too bad the cabin owners hadn't stored three longboards. Still, shortboards were better than swimming.

As they passed a large kelp bed floating along like an island, Valerie suddenly called out, "Otters!"

Jake saw them, cuddled up in their seaweed raft as if napping, sunbathing, and storm-wave surfing were all the same to them. "They'd rather be here than on shore in a storm, but they don't like whitecaps," he said.

"They're cute!" Valerie said.

Jake smiled and nodded in agreement.

After a while, Peter pointed at a crescent beach

northeast of them. "Aim for that bay while we can still see it!" he said.

For another hour, they stroked against the raging sea, saying little, concentrating only on staying together. Their arms and shoulders began to sag. Their paddling slowed little by little. At times, they could see nothing ahead; even the shore disappeared. Gale-force winds clawed at the waves, sometimes exploding them right in front of the surfers' faces. Those moments reminded Jake of being in a snow-storm whiteout. But now and again, the rain would let up, a cloud would move, and a watery peak would lift them to where they could catch a momentary glimpse of trees. Each time this happened, the shore was closer, and Jake took heart. Besides the sore shoulders, he was really starting to feel the cold, even with the constant exercise. It didn't help that they'd had so little to eat for two days.

He was concentrating on maneuvering near Valerie when Peter's voice came above the wind and crashing waves.

"The *Adrienne*!" Peter screamed, gesturing wildly.

Had he lost his mind? Jake looked left and right, scouting hard from the top of the next few surges. He could see nothing. But Peter was sprinting ahead like a crazy man.

"Peter, don't lose us!" Jake shouted, paddling as

close to Valerie as he could.

"I saw it too," Valerie called. "For a tiny second, before clouds came again. Up an inlet, Jake. A fishing boat was next to it."

"Which way?" Jake demanded, nearly swallowing a mouthful of saltwater that blew into his face as he spoke.

Valerie shook her head in confusion and clung to her board tightly as a wave shoved her hard away from him.

"We have to stay together!" Jake shouted, but the two-story waves on which they were bobbing like corks were in control now. Although the nearing shore revealed itself in peek-a-boo bursts of visibility, the mystery inlet hiding the *Adrienne*, if Peter and Valerie hadn't been hallucinating, was nowhere in sight. Even if it had been, the pitching ocean seemed to have its own mind about where it was going to push its human flotsam. Jake could only hope they were still aimed at that crescent beach. Everywhere else, it seemed, the surf crashed on jagged, van-sized rocks, a death sentence to any surfer. Then again, Jake reflected, if they didn't land soon, hypothermia would assign a different kind of death sentence.

Jake figured they'd been in the water for close to two hours when the rain eased up and the clouds over the land immediately ahead parted a mere crack, revealing a cave fronted by a strip of sand. At first glance, the sandy spot looked like a possible landing site.

"We're going to make it!" Jake shouted happily.

Peter, stroking beside him, looked less sure. Valerie, momentarily well ahead of both, began stroking so hard she resembled a swimmer in an Olympic butterfly-stroke competition.

"No, Valerie!" Peter cried out, startling Jake. "It's too narrow and rocky!"

Jake squinted and saw that Peter might be right. Then, shifting his gaze slightly northward up the shore, he saw clouds part to reveal a glimpse of the crescent beach for which they'd been aiming.

"Peter!" Jake said excitedly, pointing at the beach.

Peter nodded, then turned toward Valerie.

Jake saw that she was startlingly far ahead now and heading straight for the shore break like a mad-woman. He looked at the mini-beach in front of the cave again. Surely she could see that it was too narrow a tongue to hit, and the surf too rough to ride with any precision. Why aim for the cave's miniscule beach when the safe beach was such a short distance away? Her larger board would make it easier for her to catch a wave, but harder for her to maneuver once she was on it—a dangerous combination for such a tiny land-ing site. The waves exploding on the sharp reefs either side of the cave would surely dash her to pieces. Hadn't she looked left to see the safer beach? He glanced back toward the crescent beach, only to see that the clouds had obscured it once again, like theater curtains pulled open and closed.

"Valerie!" he screamed again, and Peter joined in. To follow her would be to commit to what she was about to attempt. Nancy's training had drilled into them that when trying to rescue someone, you must guard your own safety; otherwise you can make matters far worse.

He thought she had heard them, but she was ignoring them. She was fixated on that cave. Oh, no, Jake groaned. Was she thinking it was a burial cave? That girl is going to kill herself trying to reach a burial cave in thirty-foot surf, he thought, horrified. As if her obsession with artifacts hadn't caused enough trouble.

He screamed at her again and again, until his throat was sore. Still she paddled ahead, drawing closer and closer to the killer waves that would fling her onto the rocks.

"Jake." Peter had drawn up as close to Jake as the explosive surges around them would allow. "Let her go. She's not listening. Maybe she hasn't seen the other beach. Or maybe she's so desperate to get on dry land that she's not thinking clearly. Let's make sure we land safely. Then we can rescue her."

Jake shook his head vigorously. "We can't let her go. She won't make it."

"Exactly. Nor will either of us if we go after her."

Jake felt his stomach clench up, felt pains rake his chest. He knew Peter was right, but he couldn't turn and paddle away.

"Valerie, hold up," he screeched hysterically. His hands began clawing the water to pull himself after her.

15 Stalling for the Barrel

Before Jake could reach the danger zone—where the waves were rearing up and hurling themselves toward the cave—Peter sprinted after him. It took only a minute for Peter to deliberately slam his board into Jake's. As Jake turned, wild-eyed, Peter clenched a fist around Jake's leash cord.

"I won't let go," Peter warned. "You will not follow her." For a second, Peter was afraid Jake would release the Velcro strap that held the leash to his ankle and try to swim in, or kick at Peter to escape the hold. But the fire went out of Jake's eyes and he slumped on his board.

"She might still change her mind at the last second," Peter coaxed, though he knew it was already too late. "Or her longboard might let her pull it off. Your shortboard won't." Nobody could pull off what she was trying on any board, in Peter's opinion, but he wasn't about to say so. The girl was insane, was all he could think. "It's not too late for us to surf in on the good beach and run down to help her," Peter tried again, waiting for Jake to turn his board. *Or retrieve her body*, he refrained from saying.

Jake nodded and began pulling the water with his strong shoulders, then turned north as Peter had insisted. Peter followed, relieved, but the relief was short-lived as they reached their chosen stretch of shore minutes later.

Like Jake, Peter turned his board toward the crescent beach and waited impatiently. He could feel his heart pumping as hard as the waves hitting the shore. The open-ocean swells that they'd paddled through were standing up to their full height as they charged toward the sand. He guessed they were reaching thirty feet or more as they crested and bombed onto the beach. He'd never surfed three-story waves, had no idea if he could pull this off. The entire ocean around him seemed to be mental. He had no business being here. He must be cracked to think he'd make it in without injury. But he'd also never felt so determined to ride a wave in clean. He closed his eyes and tried to "feel" the right wave coming, the way Jake often did.

As the waves beneath him rose and fell, he felt terrified, excited, and desperate to ride, all in one. He heard a whistle, knew it was Jake's signal. He didn't need to be psychic, after all; he'd brought a psychic with him. That seemed like a good idea when dealing with psycho waves. He decided to trust Jake's call. He looked behind, saw it coming, committed himself to take it. As his arms worked the water, the mini-tsunami picked him up and launched him forward with an acceleration surely no one but astronauts had ever felt. Its shocking power gave him a rush.

Somehow—he had no idea how—he managed to get into the wave. He brought his board under him as he free-fell down the face. More amazingly, he managed to stay on his feet as his board smacked the water in the well of the wave, his board's fins and rails quivering with speed. So far, so good, but as the wall behind him grew as tall as a house, he felt terror surge through his veins. Being tumbled by this titan would require an extra set of lungs, even if he weren't knocked senseless before he ran out of air.

"Kill or be killed" shot into his mind. He knew what he had to do. Summoning all his nerve, he punched his arm deeply into the wall, hung on like it was a handbrake, and took the terrible risk of stalling in this mammoth cylinder. Would Jake and Valerie try it, too? He deeply regretted telling Valerie about this move and tried to send her a telepathic message not to try it in front of that cave, even though he knew it was probably too late. Jake, on the other hand, just might pull it off, he hoped.

Miraculously, the barrel closed over him without collapsing, played him like a pea in a peapod. At any second, he expected the hammer to come down, but the eyeball of light ahead never winked. As he hurtled toward it, he pulled his arm out of the wave and shot ahead even faster, gunning for the opening as the wave collapsed behind him. A split second later, he felt himself emerging, spit out almost gently by the slowing tube. Heart in his throat, he carved a turn, straightened out, and slowed as the menacing mountain of water melted to a foamy ridge that sped him like a water skier to the beach.

He leapt off his board and turned to see Jake facedown, stunned and gasping, in the impact zone, his board dancing behind him on the end of its leash. Peter sprinted in, grabbed Jake under his armpits, and pulled him up and out of there just before the next mallet of water fell. As both were shoved into the sand by the advancing breaker, Peter kept his hold on Jake. Moving fast, he pulled Jake up again and guided him to higher ground between wave slams.

"I got thrashed," Jake said, coughing and spluttering, as if he needed to explain.

"But you got in," Peter reassured him. "Need to catch your breath, or ready to run?"

Jake needed no further prompting. Gripping their boards, they raced up the beach, then headed south along it toward Valerie's cave until it turned to sharp rocks and slippery logs. Ignoring how the rocks cut through his neoprene boots, heedless of how many times he fell and had to pick himself up again, Peter jumped, ran, and climbed along the gnarly shoreline.

When he came to an impassable section, he hesitated. But Jake did not. A split second after a wave crashed, Jake leapt down from the rocks, sprinted through the soup, and climbed the wet cliff fast. Had he been less than a breath ahead of the next incoming roller, it would have ripped him from the wall and flung him out to sea.

"Jake!" Peter shouted. "That was stupid. Totally stupid. Slow down."

"Stupid was letting Valerie get away," Jake replied. Peter gritted his teeth and followed Jake's lead, allowing Jake to give him a hand up at the crucial moment. Although Peter's fear of heights was slowing him, with Jake's help, he moved higher up the cliff face and clambered around the corner until the two were sitting on top of the cave's roof. There they perched on rocks, shaking, as they spotted two halves of a longboard tossed viciously again and again on the rocks below.

Peter's eyes searched the shore rocks, the tiny beach, and the water for a body. No sign of Valerie. But during a brief lull between wave sets, they spotted her.

She was clinging to a pinnacle of rock offshore, a barnacle-encrusted formation as tall as a small sailboat's mast. It had a large crack into which she had inserted a leg: the only thing holding her in place. Her other leg looked unnaturally limp and twisted. He wondered if it might be broken. Her shredded gloves and bloodied palms had only a tentative hold. With every crashing tower of water, that hold was being tested. She was being battered, bruised, and half-choked.

"Valerie!" Jake and Peter shouted in unison.

She turned her face toward them. Even from that distance, Peter could see that one cheek was bruised. She looked somewhere between panic and defeat. Peter's mind raced. The storm was offering them a lull and the tide was going out, but they couldn't wait for the water to recede all the way to the base of her rock. She might well pass out before then, even if the waves didn't rip her off her rock and finish dashing her on the shore rubble. Before Peter could form a plan, Jake grabbed both their boards and started down the other side of the cave. "Follow me," he ordered.

Peter stood and followed him—fighting his urge to look down as he clung to handholds during the descent to the cave's front entrance. Then he followed Jake along a rocky arm that reached out and past Valerie's rock like a jetty. Peter figured out what Jake was up to before they reached the tip of the arm.

He didn't like it, but he wasn't going to stop him.

"I'll move back to shore to be there when you need me," he said.

Jake nodded, then jumped into the water holding both their boards, one atop the other. Peter, throat tight, retraced his steps along the jetty toward the cave's entrance, turning every few seconds to watch Jake get pounded as he worked his way toward Valerie.

When Jake reached Valerie's rock, he shouted, "Jump!"

Peter didn't know any girls who would have the presence of mind to plunge into crashing surf with a broken leg, without a second's hesitation and all on one command. Then again, Valerie was no ordinary girl. Stubborn as a mule, for sure, and a danger to herself and others, but gutsy and decisive when it counted.

He winced as he watched her fall. The pain must have been excruciating, capable of making her pass out. But fast as a rescue pro, Jake slipped both shortboards under her, then wound the leashes around her body like he was wrapping a gift box, careful not to actually tie them in case she needed a quick release. The instant he was finished, an avalanche of whitewater buried the two alive, then shot them forward out of the depths. Peter watched Jake cling to the back of the boards, pushing them when the waves offered some control, and merely clinging to them when they didn't. Valerie lay on the board like a hospital patient on a gurney, white-faced and gritting her teeth, holding her breath when they went under, and gasping for the air she needed when they came up. Once, a wave turned her face-down, but Jake's strong arms spun her back upright and steered her forward again in one swift move—not unlike the time he'd helped her roll her kayak beside the sea lions.

When the two came close to him, Peter jumped down from the jetty and helped haul them up the beach. He lost his footing and got washed back with them on the first try. But he managed to recover and drag Valerie up to the cave's entry with Jake's help the next round.

When Valerie went into a coughing fit, Peter turned her on her side, board and all, allowing her to vomit water without choking. She was in bad shape and shaking with cold, but she was alive and safe now, thanks mostly to Jake.

She squeezed both their hands, but it was several moments before she could speak.

"*Merci.* Sorry. I'm so sorry."

"Did you try to pull into a barrel?" Peter asked.

"*Oui,*" she said, wincing from the memory.

"Then I'm the one who's sorry," Peter said. He was sorry, but he was also annoyed with her for not listening when they'd shouted at her not to surf in here. Jake had put himself in danger rescuing her, and Peter found it hard to forgive her for that. He stole a look at Jake, where he read the same tangle of thoughts.

"What made you go for the cave?" he asked. "Did you not see the other beach or hear us?"

She hung her head. "I hear you, but I did not see other beach. I—I panicked."

"You're okay now," Jake said, squeezing her hand but looking out to sea instead of at her face.

After a minute, the boys turned to examine the cave's entrance, while Valerie seemed to fix her eyes on a fist-sized rock beside her. The cave was situated just above high tide, which meant they could retreat deeper into it for wind protection, but for some reason, Peter didn't want to.

It was Jake who finally made the suggestion.

"Do you want us to pull you up higher, Valerie, into the cave before one of us goes for help?"

"No," she said, so quickly and firmly that Peter turned to study her. Her eyes were still fastened on the rock beside her. It looked like an ordinary old rock to Peter, except for the sparkle of some mica. Mica. Rock glitter. What had that book of legends said about mica? It was supposed to be scales from the body of the two-headed serpent who guarded the entrances to "homes of the supernatural." Like burial caves.

She closed her eyes and lay there motionless. "I am enough trouble already."

Jake and Peter looked at each other.

"I'll go."

"No, I'll go."

"Both go," Valerie spoke, "in two directions. This will double chances of finding someone. Not to worry about me." She looked sad and scared but determined as she said it.

The boys locked eyes. "No way," they declared together.

"You stay here," Jake ordered Peter. Someone had to be beside Valerie in case she passed out. And Peter wasn't the best candidate for scrambling up rocky cliffs. "I'm going north. I think I saw a path off the beach where we surfed in. Maybe there's a house above the cove."

Peter nodded solemnly, and Valerie didn't object. "I'll be back soon with help," Jake promised Valerie, who smiled weakly. He extended a hand to Peter, who took it. Then Peter gripped Jake's shoulder.

"Good luck," Peter said.

16   The Villagers

Jake didn't like leaving Valerie, but without food, water, clothing, or blankets, they were all heading for trouble. Just the few minutes of sitting still at the cave's entrance had brought on heavy shivering again. Jake was determined to find help, and fast.

He mounted the last of the rocks on the beach and jumped on to hard-packed earth. It felt good to have soil beneath his feet again. That wave he'd caught had been the biggest he'd ever ridden—the most exciting ride in his life by far. He'd ridden it—really ridden it—even if not a soul had seen him. Okay, so he'd ridden it only until it had collapsed like a mining shaft cave-in and sent him sprawling, tumbling, and grinding into the sand. But he'd ridden it standing for at least ten seconds. After he'd been shoved into the beach, he could have crawled up above the break line without Peter's help, he figured, but he had been pretty dazed, for sure. There's nothing like a strong hand when you need one.

He was proud he'd managed to rescue Valerie, but that didn't eliminate a rising sense of frustration. No, he was more than frustrated. He was angry—at Valerie for her headstrong ways and selfish obsession with artifacts, and at himself for fooling himself all along about her.

"I've finally figured out who Valerie likes best," he announced to a squirrel scurrying up a tree he was passing. The squirrel paused as if waiting politely for the answer.

"Herself."

The squirrel skittered to the other side of the trunk and peeked back, as if expecting another outburst.

"Herself and artifacts." He strode through the trees, kicking a pinecone as hard as he could, found another and kicked it farther. Peter had been right about the bracelet. She'd given it to him in case it might be bad luck, and after the octopus-wrestling match, she'd been torn between feeling guilty about that and being angry over him losing her treasure. How's that for warped?

But even that hadn't stopped her from putting everyone at risk to see what she thought might be a burial cave. At least, that's what he figured. It probably wasn't even a burial cave—though it would have been if they'd had to bury her in it. He winced at how close she'd come to being killed, and felt his jaw clench.

Had she learned anything yet? Jake started to jog and launched another pinecone into the air. Well, *he* had. About not falling for a girl before spending more time figuring out what she's made of.

Jake lifted his neoprene boot to kick another pinecone, but the boot stopped in mid-air. He looked at the ground beneath his feet more closely. A path. He was on a path. That could only mean … He began running, pounding the soft path. He was running so hard minutes later that he nearly slammed into a middle-aged native woman walking around a bend in the path.

"Hello," she said, looking as startled as he was. She studied him head to toe, then looked through the trees to the ocean. "Are you a kayaker? You weren't paddling in this storm, were you? It's sixty-knot winds out there and thirty-foot swells!"

Fifteen minutes later, Jake found himself running alongside the woman, who'd identified herself as Jen, back toward Valerie's cave. A dozen villagers followed at their heels. She was pretty fit for an older woman, Jake decided. He could hardly keep pace with her. She carried a first aid kit. Behind them, her husband, Floyd, and his friends were jogging with a stretcher piled with blankets. Trailing them were men and women carrying food and water, and some children who seemed excited just to be part of the fast-paced parade. The children included a lively thirteen-year-old girl whom Jen had introduced as her daughter, Karen.

"It was insane to try a three-mile swim in open water," Karen told him, wagging a finger in his face. "Even without a storm, that was stupid, stupid, stupid! The only safe thing would've been to stay where you were."

"You're right," Jake acknowledged, though amused to be told off by someone younger than he was.

Jake stopped once or twice to sip water from the bottle they'd given him. He appreciated the shawl they'd wrapped around his shoulders and the wool hat someone had pulled over his wet hair. When they neared the cave, the villagers surged ahead of Jake. He was tired and less surefooted than the last time he'd negotiated his way down there, and they clearly knew the way. By the time he entered the cave, Valerie was surrounded by attendants and Peter was looking astonished.

"That was fast, old buddy," he said, moving to the rock on which Jen had made Jake sit. "She's cold, but hanging in there."

The boys watched Floyd take a pulse on her leg, then use a knife to slice Valerie's wetsuit off, knowing that tugging it off the broken leg would have been intolerably painful for her. A muscular young man examined her neck and back with the manner of an expert. Karen, Jen's daughter, moved over to her mother and the boys.

"That's my Uncle Gideon. He's a medic," she explained to Jake and Peter. As Jen rested a hand on Karen's shoulder, Jake noticed that the girl wore a delicate woven cedar bracelet and beaded jewelry in her ears and hair.

Hardly had her uncle finished when the women wrapped Valerie in blankets and plied her with warm tea from a thermal container, and some food and aspirin. The boys watched as four young men lifted Valerie gently onto the stretcher. She cried out once, then seemed to bite her tongue to keep herself from doing so again. Curious young children crowded around to look at her. Karen stood and shooed them away, then gently brushed strands of hair away from Valerie's forehead.

"*Encore du thé?* Will you have some more tea?" Karen asked Valerie.

Jake was amazed by her flawless French.

"*Merci,*" Valerie responded gratefully, her pale face turning to the girl. "*Vous parlez français.* You speak French."

"It's her favorite subject, besides art," Jen spoke up

proudly. "She's beyond what our local school can teach her, so she's taking it by correspondence course on the Net. But Karen, darling, let Valerie be while your uncle finishes with her."

Karen moved back to the boys and Jen, and joined her mother in pushing food and hot drinks on Jake and Peter. The two ate and drank gratefully.

"Why would you leave the island in such a storm?" Jen asked Jake as Gideon began examining Jen's leg again.

"We had no radio, no way of knowing a storm or big surf was coming," Jake said, averting his eyes from Valerie's gritted teeth.

"Do you not know the natural signs of an approaching storm?" Jen asked.

"Natural signs?" Peter asked.

"Frogs making a terrible racket. Seagulls clustered on the beaches and refusing to fly. A halo around the sun or moon, winds calming right before the storm, and red sky—"

Jake held up a hand. "We have heard that one. I guess we were just eager to get off that island," he said, feeling foolish. After all, they were supposed to be wilderness guides.

Jen smiled. "There's another phrase, 'Wind from the south brings rain in its mouth.'"

"Valerie'll like that one," Peter said.

They watched Gideon splint her leg and start dressing some of her more gaping cuts with swift, sure hands. Valerie hardly flinched during the procedure. She was one brave girl.

Jen kept peppering the boys with questions. When Jake and Peter told her about the *Adrienne* disappearing, Jake noticed a look pass between her and Floyd.

"What?" Jake pressed, hoping she might be able to tell him something helpful.

"There has been a rash of small pleasure boats and kayaks being stolen around here this summer," she said, voice low. "Each time, the owners are stranded."

"We've had several stranded boaters come to our village needing help," Karen added.

"But the thieves have never taken a yacht," Jen said.

"And have the thieves been caught? Have the owners gotten their boats back?" Peter asked.

Again, Jen and Floyd exchanged a look, as if they knew more than they were telling.

"Always they've gotten them back, usually within hours," Jen said. "The boats are being taken by joyriders —we think by local youths. They hide them only a short distance away, then disappear. No one has caught these pranksters yet."

"But we suspect who they might be," Karen said, causing her mother to frown.

"Oh," said Jake, scratching his head. "Stealing a

sixty-three-foot yacht and parking it up an inlet sure seems a big step up from hiding a kayak around a corner. It's a prank that could have killed the three of us, if there hadn't been a cabin on that island. And we don't know what situation it has put the captain and first mate in."

"I agree," Jen said, eyes cast to the floor of the cave as strong men hoisted Valerie up and began carrying her stretcher out of the cave.

"*Merci*, Jake," Valerie whispered as she passed him.

He reached out and squeezed her hand, but whatever reply he meant to make got stuck in his throat.

"Come with us and rest until the Coast Guard gets here," Karen spoke up. "Someone called them as we left the village, you know."

"Okay," said Jake, suddenly feeling very weary.

"Jake," Jen said a while later as she and the boys reached the path. Jake was walking behind Valerie's stretcher, Jen and Peter a footstep behind him. "What business were the captain and his helper on here, exactly?"

"Fishing. It was a weekend off for them," Jake replied. Something in her tone made him turn. "Why?"

"Because," Jen said, frowning, "only certain boats have been stolen by the joyriders."

"What are you saying, Jen?" Jake asked.

"Do you know what burial caves are?"

Jake stole a glance at Valerie, saw her tired eyes turn their way.

"Yes," he said.

"Of course," Peter added.

"Sometimes kayakers or tourists have been known to enter them and ..."

"... and desecrate them," Floyd inserted in a loud voice, eyes on Jake.

"What means 'desecrate'?" Valerie spoke up.

"They disturb them," Karen said quietly.

"They steal or destroy things!" Floyd said, eyes flashing.

Jake saw Valerie's face freeze. Slowly, her eyes moved to Jake's face. He felt his lips tighten and his eyes narrow before he looked away.

"So," Jake turned to Jen and Karen, "some native youths are taking and 'joyriding' the boats of disrespectful visitors when their heads are turned, to teach them a lesson. Is that what you're saying?" Jake kept his tone quiet and respectful. Beside him, Peter's mouth was hanging a little open.

Jen looked from Jake and Peter to Valerie, and back to Jake, her quick pace never slowing. "Yes, Jake. Could your captain and his helper have been involved in such activities?"

"Oh, no," Valerie said, echoed by Peter, but Jake cut them off.

"Yes, I believe they were. I know that only because I stumbled across a large brass box of native artifacts in Gavin's clothes cupboard. I thought they were replicas from the Tofino Gallery at the time, but ..."

"You never said anything about that!" Peter interrupted.

"A *large box?*" Floyd demanded, his face stormy.

"Jake ..." Valerie started.

"Shut up, Valerie! I'll tell them if I want to." He ignored her shocked face. He'd never spoken to any girl like that, let alone Valerie. But he was putting things together, and if she was to blame for the *Adrienne*'s disappearance, he wasn't going to spare her feelings at this point.

Jen was staring at Valerie as the little procession continued along the path to the village.

"Valerie's parents own a museum in France," Jake said. "Her parents may have put the captain and his first mate up to stealing artifacts for them. At least, that's what I think. You can ask Valerie when she's feeling better," he said bitterly.

"Jake," Valerie said, trying to rise on her elbow but sinking back in pain, "I know nothing of this. Why you think this is true?"

"Jake!" was all Peter could say.

"Because I saw Gavin taking notes while he talked to them at your hotel patio, the night before we left,"

Jake said. "And you and the bracelet, and then the cave. I'm not as stupid as I look, Valerie."

When she didn't answer, and Peter went quiet, he dared to look down at Valerie. He saw tears falling from her bruised face onto the stretcher. Now he felt rotten.

Jen caught Jake by the arm. "Not now, Jake. This is a discussion for later. This poor girl needs air evacuation as soon as possible."

But Valerie spoke, her voice incredulous, as her stretcher continued moving. "You think I surf to cave because I think it is burial cave?"

Jake's silence as he continued keeping pace with the stretcher seemed to give her the answer.

"Jake, I saw beach, and I want to land. I never saw beach you and Peter find. I was cold and scared, Jake. I took terrible, stupid chance. I heard you shout but did not listen. This is my fault, but I was not thinking of burial-cave artifacts. And I think you are wrong about my parents asking such thing of Gavin."

Still, Jake could not make himself say anything. He felt torn, guilty, and confused. Everyone in the group surrounding Valerie's stretcher had gone very quiet, even Karen. Only the crunch of pine needles on the path underfoot indicated that a dozen villagers were still moving beside them.

"I am interested in burial caves, yes," Valerie continued.

"But you teach me now that it is bad luck to take things." She was quiet, then looked at Jen and Floyd, as if suddenly realizing they were listening. "And wrong."

"Bad luck, wrong, *and illegal*," Floyd inserted forcefully.

"It's illegal?" Peter piped up. Jake was surprised, too.

"Since 1979 in British Columbia," Jen said more gently, "for anything pre-contact, which means from before 1846. Canada, the United States, and many other countries have similar laws. Think of all the poles, masks, and sculptures taken from aboriginal people by collectors before that law—and are still being taken, despite the law," she added. "Now there's a big move to get those back."

"Kind of like the Elgin Marbles," Jake thought aloud. "Those famous statues from ancient Greece that an English guy took way back when, and that Greece is trying to get some English museum to return now."

"Yeah," Karen spoke up. "Like, if some aliens from Mars swooped down and stole the Declaration of Independence from that museum in Washington, D.C., and then the Americans got up to Mars, I think the Americans would ask for it back."

Jake watched her mother's expression reveal a touch of amusement before turning serious again. He also saw that they were nearing the village.

Peter scratched his head. "Okay, that makes sense.

But is that what the captain and Gavin were up here for? And did someone from the village see them collecting artifacts? And Jake, are you sure Valerie's parents asked them to do it? And Valerie, do you think your parents know it's illegal?"

The last question made Jake's mind flash back to the Chambres' interest in the Japanese glass ball they had found on the beach. That was legal to take, but if it had been an artifact, would they have given it up?

"I think this maybe they do not know," Valerie said softly.

"I think," Karen said, "your boat wouldn't have disappeared if someone hadn't seen at least one of them stealing."

"That's enough from you," Floyd reprimanded his daughter harshly.

17   Helicopter Transport

Under Floyd's direction, they lay Valerie, stretcher and all, on a large table in a quiet, art-filled room of the village's community center. Karen pulled a chair up close to her head and began brushing Valerie's hair very gently, which brought a small smile to the girl's lips. The rest of the group stood hovering, as if waiting for someone's orders.

Peter watched Valerie's face take in the artwork in the room, including some woven cedar wall hangings. Then her eyes moved to Karen's bracelets and earrings.

"Pretty," she said, which lit up Karen's face.

"I made them," Karen said in French with an exuberant smile. "And Mother made most of the wall hangings here. She's an artist—she has some work at the Tofino Art Gallery—and this is our community center's art room. I'm going to be a jewelry maker."

"Karen, you've been told she needs rest," Floyd

chided his daughter. "You can stay here with Gideon if you promise not to say another word, in French or English. Hopefully, Valerie can sleep until the Coast Guard helicopter arrives. Everyone else needs to clear out of here."

The group dissipated fast, as if accustomed to taking orders from Floyd. Peter was the last to leave, his eyes on Valerie's face. She'd closed her eyes. He hoped she would sleep. Gideon was taking her pulse and Karen was adjusting her blankets.

Floyd and Jen ushered the boys to a lunchroom where people were scurrying about, piling food onto plates and pushing the boys to sit down. Peter had never been so hungry in his life. He felt capable of emptying several of the plates being set before him, but he shook his head. "Phone calls first. Jake and I have to reach Nancy Sheppard, our boss."

"Of course," Jen said, leading him to the office. Jake followed.

The boys couldn't remember where Nancy was staying, so they decided to phone Valerie's parents at the big hotel.

"Oh, Peter, we were just rushing out to the Coast Guard office," Dr. Chambre said in a husky voice. "We've only just been told of Valerie's injury. Nancy, Captain Dylan, and Gavin are in the helicopter on their way to you. Her mother and I will be at the hospital when she arrives here. The helicopter couldn't take any more people."

"Captain Dylan and Gavin?" Peter said, astonished. "They're in Tofino?"

"No, they're in the helicopter on their way from Tofino to you. They will tell you their story when they get there. The *Adrienne* was stolen, their dinghy ran out of gas, and they spent two days beating their way through the bush along the coast before a boat picked them up and brought them back to Tofino. They arrived just a few hours ago. The Coast Guard was waiting for the storm to lift enough to launch a search for you when the call came about Valerie. We are so thankful you are all alive. You can't imagine what we've been going through since the *Adrienne* didn't show up this morning. Nancy, too. How is Valerie, please, besides the broken leg?"

Peter was almost too stunned to reply, and also amazed that it was only this morning that they'd all been expected back. But of course. It was only Monday, and not much past mid-day yet. It felt like a hundred years since they'd left Tofino on Saturday morning. "Um, Valerie is good. She's sleeping now, I think. A medic is looking after her. She was very brave," Peter said, his voice catching a little as he said it. He still couldn't believe how she'd saved her own life by squeezing herself into the crook of the towering rock. Not only had she withstood the battering waves, but she'd jumped back into the storm surf, broken leg and all, trusting Jake to rescue her.

There was a pause on the end of the line. "Peter, can her mother and I speak with her?"

Peter covered the receiver with one hand and asked Jen, "Can her parents speak with her?"

Jen shook her head firmly. "Sorry, she's asleep," Peter said. "If the helicopter is on its way here, she'll be at the Tofino hospital in less than an hour. She's okay, Dr. Chambre. Really she is. Thanks for telling us Captain Dylan and Gavin are okay."

As he hung up, he was bombarded with questions from Jake, Jen, and Floyd, but he held up his arm. "Food!" he declared. "Food first, stories while we're eating!"

They'd barely finished eating and talking at a frenetic pace when the deafening noise of a helicopter landing nearby caused them to jump up and run. Hardly had the giant Coast Guard bird set down when Nancy leapt out, head low under the swirling rotors, followed by the captain, Gavin, and a man with a medical bag. The captain, though fresh-shaven, was wearing clothing that didn't fit quite right. Perhaps they were borrowed, Peter thought. Gavin was better dressed and had clearly taken the time to comb some gel into his hair.

Nancy's face was a little drawn, but her embrace was warm and full. Peter squirmed when she held on too long. As she released each of the boys, she shook her head. "You two are something. Every trip you take, you put gray hairs on my head."

"Ha! You have a long way to go to catch up to me," Jen joked, extending her hand. "You must be Nancy."

Before Jen could greet the rest of the newcomers, Floyd and his helpers came hurrying out of the center carrying Valerie on her stretcher. Peter watched as the doctor took over, blocking everyone from saying goodbye to her. Captain Dylan winced as he watched Valerie moved. Valerie waved at the boys and Nancy as she was lifted into the 'copter. Everyone backed away as the machine roared and lifted away.

Gavin ran a sleeve across his sweating forehead and watched the helicopter disappear in the clearing sky.

"Just a broken leg and bruises?" the captain queried Jen, as everyone introduced themselves and he shook hands all around. "She'll be alright, then?"

"I think she'll be fine," Jen reassured him. "But it's a good thing we got to her when we did. Jake here risked his life to save her," she added soberly, placing a hand on Jake's shoulder.

"You're a good lad," the captain said, then eyed Peter. "Both of you. If Gavin were half as responsible, we'd have had enough gas in the dinghy to do a second search for you. We did comb both islands, you know"—he jabbed a finger west at the faraway humps of land—"but when we returned to fuel up, the whole dang boat had disappeared. That sure scared the stuffing out of us."

He paused and looked at all the faces turned to him. "Now, who's going to tell me why you three didn't stick within sight of the *Adrienne* in the first place, and where you got to?"

Peter and Jake started speaking all at once. Within ten minutes, they'd spilled the entire story of the tunnel, domed cave, island, and surf adventure.

"And we know where the *Adrienne* is," Peter added.

"Yes, we know too," Gavin said, nodding. "The captain of a seine boat called it in to the Coast Guard. That's why the Coast Guard gave us a lift up here. The seine boat captain reported that the *Adrienne* sheltered from the storm with no damage, thanks to the protected inlet where the thieves so thoughtfully left it." His sarcasm was aimed at ingratiating himself with the captain, Peter thought. But it prompted a few villagers, those who'd heard the earlier conversation about Gavin and his box of artifacts, to exchange looks when they thought Peter wasn't looking.

"Can't wait to get my hands on them," Captain Dylan muttered, fists clenching and unclenching. "I'll teach 'em to take my property for a spin, I will."

There was an awkward silence from the crowd. Peter cleared his throat. He was about to ask about the box Jake had mentioned, when Gavin spoke.

"Turns out the *Adrienne* is barely around the corner from where we landed the dinghy on the mainland after searching for you. We had to row the dinghy to shore the last fifteen minutes because we ran out of fuel."

"Outta fuel 'cause of yer incompetence!" the captain roared at Gavin.

"But we didn't know the inlet was there, let alone that the *Adrienne* had been parked there," Gavin continued, bravely ignoring the captain's outburst. "If we'd hiked north instead of south, we'd have found it in ten minutes." He shook his head and brushed a cricket from his jacket cuff.

"Instead of two days of roughin' it!" the captain inserted. "I never want to see another salal bush in my life," he added. "At least we finally got picked up by a boat waiting out the storm in an inlet we couldn't have crossed."

"But you had some emergency supplies from the dinghy," Nancy spoke up.

Good thing, Peter thought. But he was wondering how to bring the conversation around to the box of artifacts, as he was sure the villagers were waiting for him or Jake to do.

"So we'll be making our way to the *Adrienne* now," the captain said. "Soon as we know she's good and the weather has settled, we'll radio you here and get set to pick up you boys and Nancy for Tofino, yes?" He tugged on his cap, ran his gray eyes around the group.

"Sounds good," Nancy ruled.

"I can lead you to it," a girl's voice offered. Everyone turned to look at Karen. "There's a path to that inlet. It's a half-hour walk. You'll need someone to show you the way."

"Not without Gideon along. And the men will want to eat something first," Jen insisted, looking sternly at her daughter.

"And who are you?" Gavin asked Karen, looking her up and down.

"Karen," she said, eyes narrowed as she extended her hand to both men. "Jen and Floyd's daughter." She shot a glance at Peter as if preparing him for her next comment. "Please tell us about the box of artifacts Jake tells us you have onboard your boat."

"Karen!" Jen snapped, hand moving to her mouth.

"Let her!" Floyd ordered his wife.

Gavin turned an astonished stare from Karen to Jake.

"I, um," Jake began. Then Peter watched him draw himself up, scan Peter's and the villagers' faces for support, and return Gavin's accusing glare. "I found it in your clothes cupboard when I was looking for rags to change the oil."

"Box of artifacts?" Captain Dylan's deep voice questioned as he took in the faces of the gathering, then let his gaze settle on Gavin. "What's this about?"

"If Gavin has a box of artifacts stolen from sites around here," Peter turned to the captain, "that explains why the *Adrienne* was stolen. Someone around here— Jen and Floyd don't know who—has been hijacking boats from people they've seen raiding burial caves and other archaeological sites. You don't know anything about Gavin's artifacts, Captain Dylan?"

The big man's face hardened and his eyes seared into Gavin. "Burial caves? Is that what that cave was you disappeared into when I was fishing? I wondered what the blazes kept you so long!" His face was a study in temper control.

"I—I …" Gavin began, but under the gaze of the villagers, he abandoned whatever he was about to say.

"It's illegal!" the captain roared at his first mate, wagging a finger in his face. "If you've been using my *Adrienne* to find and store illegal goods, Gavin Kelly …"

Peter watched Gavin cringe and Floyd cross his arms. Karen, with a trace of triumph on her face, was half hiding behind her mother, whose face was creased with worry.

"Jake, Peter," Nancy spoke up as she moved forward from the crowd, "why don't you go with the captain, Gavin, Karen, and Gideon to the *Adrienne*? The rest of us will wait here until you return with the box." She gave the captain a firm nod and Gavin a dismissive look. "I'll notify the clients in Tofino that we'll likely depart from Tofino for Seattle tomorrow morning, just one day late. Minus the Chambres, of course," she added quietly.

"Yes, Karen and Gideon, go," Floyd agreed as Karen's uncle appeared. "We'll take care of some matters here before you return," he added, taking Jen's hand and turning to all the villagers, whose eyes were on him.

18   Brass Box

The forest smelled fresh in the aftermath of the storm as Jake padded silently behind Karen and her ragtag collection of adventurers, but already the warming afternoon sun was making the air close and sticky. Karen, excited by her role as guide, glided along a forest path as confidently as a ship's bow figurine. Gideon padded silently behind her. Jake followed them at a respectful distance, keeping his eyes straight ahead so he wouldn't have to meet Gavin's eyes. Peter was whistling as he walked immediately behind Jake. At the rear, the captain had slowed his long gait to keep stride with Gavin, who was negotiating the path as stiffly as a convict already in irons. The two were talking in low tones.

"Step on it or we'll lose our guides, old buddy," Peter teased him. "You're dragging."

The truth was, Jake was trying to eavesdrop on the

men's mumbles behind them, but it wasn't working. So he quickened his step, reflecting that if the captain weren't with them, Gavin would probably be tearing a strip off his hide about snooping in his closet. That Karen was a bit devious for a kid, confronting Gavin publicly like that.

"Could've used some more lunch," Jake replied to imply that his slowness stemmed from hunger.

"Seemed to me you polished off plenty," Peter said, snatching some berries from nearby bushes and handing them to Jake.

"Hey, guys, aren't you going to offer me some?" Karen said, having slowed to join them, Gideon standing silently to one side. "Bet I know what my mom and dad are doing right now."

"What?" the boys said together.

"Smoking out the hijackers."

"Yeah? How will they do that?" Jake asked.

"Well, in a village our size, everyone knows everyone, so we pretty much already suspect who has been doing what. The elders will call a council meeting, and by the time they're done, whoever has been taking the boats will want to confess."

"Sounds interesting," Jake offered. "Then what?"

"I'm guessing we'll find out when we get back," she said with a toss of her hair. "So, there's your boat. Big one," she said, eyebrows raised. "Can't wait for my tour. But how're we going to get aboard?"

The sloop was anchored a several-minute swim from where they were standing on the inlet's shore.

"We need the dinghy to get to her unless someone wants to swim," Captain Dylan declared. "Gavin, you want to swim, or you want to walk another ten minutes and fetch that dinghy back here with me?"

Jake, Peter, Karen, and Gideon sat down, chatted, and tossed pinecones into the water until the men returned with the dinghy and paddled them out to the sloop. Gavin managed to give Jake the evil eye as he stroked through the water.

Once aboard, the captain moved agilely to check everything, while Gavin refueled the dinghy. "Don't go touching anything in the wheelhouse in case we need fingerprints," the captain ordered. Then he led the group down the companionway to Gavin's clothes cupboard.

When Gavin hesitated, Captain Dylan used a strong arm to push him forward. "Open it." Gavin pulled the cupboard door open, got down on his knees and hauled the brass box out from under its thick camouflage of rags with difficulty as everyone moved closer. He wrestled it onto a nearby bunk and looked about, as if needing orders to open it.

"Can I?" Karen asked, stepping forward and lifting the lid without waiting for permission.

Silence fell as everyone stared at the contents in the box.

"This couldn't be all from one site. How long did it take you to gather all these?" she asked Gavin, her face flushed.

"A couple of months," he said, as if torn between pride and distress. "I'm sure a museum would appreciate them if that's where you'd like ..." he added, trailing off.

Karen snapped the box shut and turned to Gideon. "I hope we can carry this in the dinghy. It's heavy."

"It'll fit," Jake ruled.

"I'll help carry it," Peter offered.

Half an hour later, the dinghy and its six passengers puttered to shore beside what appeared to be an empty village. But Karen and Gideon led them directly to the community center, Jake and Peter toting the heavy box between them. "They'll all be in here," Karen predicted.

Sure enough, the hall was full, with many elderly people seated around three boys no older than Jake and Peter. The three boys' faces glistened with sweat, and their faces didn't indicate they were happy to be the center of attention. Nancy was sitting beside Jen. She nodded at the boys as they spotted her.

Floyd rose to usher in the party from the *Adrienne*. Karen squeezed in beside her mother, who put her arm around her.

"The boat is fine," the captain said. "No damage. We can still dust the wheelhouse for fingerprints."

"No need for that." Floyd motioned them to join the gathering. "These boys have confessed, and they have heard from our elders about traditions and how to honor them. Now we need to hear from Gavin."

Gavin's eyes shot to the door, and he looked ready to move for it. Captain Dylan's hand landed gently on his back. "I'm sure Gavin would be interested in participating," he said in a baritone voice that seemed to reverberate off the walls of the room.

Jake and Peter lowered the little trunk to the floor, and people moved to make room for it in the center of the circle.

"I, well, I actually did know it was illegal to take artifacts," Gavin began, hands fluttering until he stuffed them into his pockets. "But I've always been interested in them."

"So have we," Floyd said dryly. Jake watched Nancy's eyes move around the room to take in everyone's expressions.

Gavin's hands fumbled with the latch, then he lifted the small trunk's lid. Everyone pressed forward to look. When one of the youth's hands shot out to touch a bracelet, an elder reached forward to tap his arm gently, prompting him to withdraw the hand quickly.

"It's yours, of course," Gavin said lamely to Floyd,

looking pained as he took a last look at his treasures.

"The law dictates up to a $500,000 fine for removing these from their locations," Floyd intoned, looking from Nancy to Gavin to the captain. "And the captain here could charge our youths with stealing his boat. Or," he looked around the gathering in his commanding way, "we could all agree to live with the outcomes agreed upon here."

"I think we should agree to what you suggest," Gavin spoke up unexpectedly.

Jake studied Gavin's face, which was directed on the boys crouched in the center.

"Agreed," the captain said, standing to his full height. Nancy nodded her approval at him.

"The elders will determine how many hours of community work the boys should do," Floyd continued.

"Then I will not press charges on these boys," the captain replied, his eyes on them fiercely, "although they should realize that their actions put several people's lives at risk this week. And rather than fire Gavin," he continued, gray eyes moving to his hunched first mate, "I'm inclined to deduct a portion of his pay-check for the next six months as a symbolic gesture of paying off that fine."

Jake watched Gavin stiffen and his frown deepen.

"Or," Floyd said, looking at the boys in the center of the circle, then at the elders, "if no fine is levied, perhaps that money could go towards outfitting a youth center in our community."

Several of the elders nodded at Floyd. One smiled. The youths looked at one another. One whispered, "yesss" under his breath.

"Sounds good to me," the captain said.

"And me," Gavin said, shoulders slightly more relaxed. "I'm sorry."

"We'd like to thank you for helping rescue Valerie," Jake spoke up, his eyes moving to Gideon, the medic, who nodded at him in return.

"And feeding us and notifying the Coast Guard and all that," Peter added as Nancy smiled.

"Well, then," Floyd said, moving to close the lid of the brass box, "speaking of feeding and the Coast Guard, I believe Jen has some more food on, and the Coast Guard's latest report indicates that it would be safe for the *Adrienne* to leave for Tofino in another hour."

"With a stop at the cabin to replace supplies, maybe leave some money, and get the dive gear back if the tide is right," Jake suggested.

"Alright, food!" Peter said as he high-fived his buddy. Out of the corner of his eye, Jake saw the disciplined youths also high-fiving, more soberly, and an elder patting them on their heads.

19   Au Revoir

J ake felt a little out of place walking up Tofino's main street with a bouquet of flowers, but with Peter moving alongside him carrying a second bouquet, maybe it wasn't so embarrassing.

As they entered the Tofino hospital, a nurse beamed at them. "Now, you two wouldn't be here for Miss Valerie Chambre, would you?"

Jake nodded.

"Goodness! That girl has more flowers in her room than a greenhouse!" The nurse motioned the boys to follow her as she bustled up the hallway.

"Jake, Peter," Valerie beamed, looking as radiant as a bed-ridden hospital patient with a raised leg in a cast could. Someone had helped her wash and brush her hair, had even wound her string of beads into it. The evening's rosy sunset was shining on her face, and the white pillows propped around her showed off her dark hair. Flowers filled the room. They must be from other members of the kayaking trip, Jake realized.

Jake couldn't stop his pulse quickening as she held her hand out to him.

"You look good," Jake said.

She laughed. "Good?"

"Well, considering."

"Yes, considering." She smiled. "My parents are taking break from making too much fuss here. The trip back on *Adrienne* was okay?"

"Entirely boring," Peter joked. "No waves to speak of. Just the way we wanted it. I guess the storm finally blew itself out. Unless you account for the new storm between the captain and Gavin."

Valerie nodded. Then she turned to Jake. "Jake, I must tell you that my parents tell me they never tell Gavin to find them artifacts. He tell them about his collection he already has and ask what they like. They not understand they are not his to sell. Then he makes list of what they say they like. Nothing else happen. I explain to them today that they were not ours to take."

Not ours to take, thought Jake. *Like Valerie. I guess she was never mine—never really interested in Peter or me in the way we wanted.*

"Jake?" Valerie was looking at him curiously.

"Sorry, Valerie, I heard you. And I'm sorry I thought what I did about your parents without finding out first."

"Is okay. So, will captain keelhaul Gavin?" she asked with a smile.

"Or ask him to take a long walk off a short plank," Peter inserted.

"If I were Gavin," came Nancy's voice as she strode into the room, "I'd prefer either of those to working under the captain's nose the next few months, never mind the docked paycheck."

Jake, Peter, and Valerie chuckled as they turned her way.

"So, Valerie," Nancy continued, pausing at the foot of the hospital bed, "visiting hours are nearly over, and we lift anchor in the morning. I am sorry you and your parents are unable to continue onboard the *Adrienne*, but you have certainly had an adventurous holiday. Your parents seem happy to be able to stay here for a few more days. I hope you've had a chance to say goodbye to Jake and Peter."

Valerie's smile, which had seemed so bright until now, faded.

"No, Nancy. This is too difficult," she said softly.

"I understand," Nancy said gently, moving closer and squeezing Valerie's arm. "I will say goodbye myself, then, and leave you another ten minutes with them. It has been a pleasure knowing you, Valerie. You are welcome to return next summer to do another trip with Sam's Adventure Tours—on us."

This re-lit Valerie's face. "You can count on this," she said. "You have very good junior guides."

Nancy laughed, gave the boys a "ten minutes only" look, and exited the hospital room.

"Young men," the nurse said, popping her head in as Nancy disappeared, "ten minutes only. This surfer girl needs her beauty rest."

Peter coughed. "Valerie, you can email us anytime. You can even email us in French. I'll get Jake to translate."

"You trust me to tell you what she really says about you?" Jake teased.

"But of course, old buddy. They don't make guys like us back in France, do they Valerie? She'll miss the West Coast and be back in no time. Right, Val?"

"*Oui*, Peter," Valerie said, eyes crinkling with laughter.

"Then listen up, 'cause these are almost the only French words I remember," Peter said, leaning forward to kiss her on alternate cheeks, three times like in France. "*Au revoir. Peut-être je vais te visiter en France.*"

"*Oui*, Peter, come visit me in France," Valerie replied. Peter nodded, then he was gone, out the door, vanished.

"Goodbye, Valerie," Jake tried to say casually as he squeezed her hand.

"Jake," Valerie said, eyes on his, "you saved my life."

He shrugged.

"You also teach me how to be better person," she said.

He looked at her curiously. She held her arm up, and he saw she was wearing a woven cedar bracelet. She pushed it closer to him.

"This is gift from Karen. You see picture on it?"

Jake looked closer, saw a two-headed serpent neatly inked atop the woven bracelet. "Sisiutl."

"Karen says Sisiutl is not from her people or the Nuu-chah-nulth area, where we were. Sisiutl is Kwakiutl, more north. But she knows about Sisiutl and after I tell her about how we read the legend, she says rock that save me has two heads, like Sisiutl. She gives me this for good luck."

Jake nodded. The split rock that nearly killed her, but also saved her. The rock guarding the entrance to the cave.

"It's nice." He needed to get away. He hated goodbyes.

"She making you cedar bracelet too."

"Me?" Jake was confused.

"I ask her, Jake. For your good luck. And to thank you."

Jake nodded. It was time to let go of her hand, but he couldn't. The hand tightened around his, drew him closer. The eyes drew him closer still. She gave him a goodbye kiss. Not on the cheek.

"Ahem," said the nurse.

Jake straightened up. Valerie's hand let go. She pointed to the window. "Look, Jake. Red sky."

"Red sky at night, sailor's delight."

"It will be good day tomorrow. I will be here thinking of you."

"*Soigne toi bien.* Get well soon, Valerie. Take care of yourself. And keep in touch," he said. "*Au revoir.*"

Peter was waiting in the reception area.

"So," he said, eyebrows raised, "down to nine clients again. None to fight over. But we can still dazzle them with our knowledge, impress them with our muscles, and save the occasional gray-haired damsel in distress."

"And on our time off, we can catch waves," Jake joined in.

"I can catch waves. Can you catch waves?"

"You should have seen me catch that wave …" Jake enthused.

"I didn't see you, Jake. And can you stall in a barrel?"

"No, but can you wrestle an octopus?"

"With one hand behind my back while stalling in a barrel."

Jake was trying not to laugh. "Has anyone ever told you that you talk too much and have an over-inflated sense of self?"

"Frequently. But you put up with me 'cause there's never a dull moment when we hang together."

Jake sighed. "What's our next adventure?"

"Hey, we have a week onboard a sixty-three-foot yacht to mull that over."

"And we get to stay tonight in a five-star hotel equipped with a swimming pool, sauna, and hot tub." Jake could hardly wait.

"Courtesy of the Chambres," Peter confirmed. "For services rendered in saving a damsel in distress."

"Guess we should do that more often."

"Sounds good to me. Next time, though, we need two damsels." Peter raised his eyebrows and ran a hand through his curls.

"That's not the same as a two-headed serpent?"

"No, Jake, it's not. Grow up, hey?"

"After you, old buddy."